THE TREE AND
THE VINE

THE TREE AND THE VINE

Dola de Jong

Translated from the Dutch by
Kristen Gehrman

TRANSIT BOOKS

Published by Transit Books
2301 Telegraph Avenue, Oakland, California 94612
www.transitbooks.org

ISBN: 978-1-945492-34-1 (paperback)
LIBRARY OF CONGRESS CONTROL NUMBER: 2020933970

DESIGN & TYPESETTING
Justin Carder

DISTRIBUTED BY
Consortium Book Sales & Distribution
(800) 283-3572 | cbsd.com

Printed in the United States of America

9 8 7 6 5 4 3 2 1

Nederlands
letterenfonds
dutch foundation
for literature

This publication has been made possible with financial
support from the Dutch Foundation for Literature.

1

I MET ERICA IN 1938 at the home of a mutual acquaintance, a superficial acquaintance, as far as I was concerned, and not someone I wanted to invest a lot of time in. Wies and I had spent six weeks lying next to each other in a hospital room, and our time together didn't inspire me to get to know her any better. After a month and a half, I'd had my fill. Wies is the type of woman who, once she gets another woman to herself, casts out a net of feminine solidarity, and the only way to escape is to run away as fast as you can, but that wasn't an option for me at the time. She had thick skin, typical of her kind, and my lack of enthusiasm and feigned drowsiness only seemed to make her want to confide in me even more. After being released from the hospital two weeks before I was, she visited me often and brought me all kinds of flowers and treats.

I felt like I couldn't completely ignore her after that, so every now and then I made a point to accept one of her many invitations. I had an aversion to offending people back then, not that I can blame myself for it anymore—it was at her house that I met Erica. It was a warm summer evening, and I decided to ride my bicycle over to Wies's to pay my obligatory visit. To be honest, I was hoping she wouldn't be home, that I'd be able to just drop a note in the mailbox, and my duty would be done. But the door opened as soon as I rang the bell, and I once again found myself trapped.

Erica was lying on the couch near the open doors to the balcony. When Wies introduced us, she seemed to hesitate for a moment as to whether she should stand up or stay lying down. My outstretched hand decided for her; with an agile swing of the legs, she slid off the couch. I was instantly attracted to her and forgot all about the burden of my visit. Even now, after all these years, I still picture Erica gliding off the couch and taking my hand. Her face was round and youthful, but there was something old about her mouth, as if it were being pulled down by the corners. She had a penetrating, somewhat melancholic look in her brown eyes. She was wearing sandals, bright blue wool socks, a pleated skirt and a red sports blouse unbuttoned at the neck. Her blond hair had been cut short with a fringe poking out at the neck that made her look like a boy in need of a haircut. In other words, she was dressed like a member of the Socialist Youth, a crowd I'd never felt very comfortable around. We had a couple of those girls at the office, and I stayed out of their way. But Erica seemed different. That first evening, I got the impression that she dressed this way because she was struggling to accept her own adulthood. Later, I realized that her clothes were really just the simplest solution to her financial stalemate. But I don't attach much value to that discovery anymore either.

That night, at Wies's house, Erica's life became part of my own. It was a chance encounter, and I've often wondered what my life would've been like if we'd never met. For a long time,

I saw myself as an innocent bystander, but I now know that I changed my course for Erica. Whether my life would've been better or happier without her—who knows? I certainly don't.

Within a month of meeting each other, we moved in together. I'd already been planning to move for a while. I'd had enough of landladies, and my women's boardinghouse had started to feel more like a boarding school. I'd been living there since I left home after my father died, and it was only out of laziness that I hadn't left yet. Erica, on the other hand, had had a decisive row with her mother and was looking for a new place to live.

The rental contract for the apartment on the Prinsengracht was in my name. Erica was working as a journalist for *Nieuws Post* at the time and earning a novice's salary. Her position was just one step up from a volunteer—the bait they used in those days to lure young people in and exploit them for all they were worth. Before that, she'd spent two years volunteering at a local newspaper and sponging off her mother's income. Now she was stuck paying "Ma" back. It was a vicious cycle, and a fate shared by many young people during the depression.

The way that Erica talked about her mother made me laugh that first year. No matter what happened, she'd find the humor in it. At the time, I didn't understand what was behind all her joking around about Ma; I simply enjoyed her talent for storytelling.

"Ma called," she'd holler on her way up the stairs to our apartment after work. "The General is going on vacation, and Ma can't go." Once upstairs, she'd give an embellished report of all her mother's complaints about the retired warhorse whose household she commandeered.

That first year with Erica on the Prinsengracht was full of surprises. Looking back, I have no idea how I accepted her often peculiar behavior with so little resistance. Of course, I saw her struggles and conflicts, but in those years, it was as if they were projected like silhouettes on a white screen—only later, after I had some insight into Erica's background, did the images take on form and color. In those first twelve months together, I was spared the agony of understanding, simply because I was predisposed to restraint. We'd decided to each lead our own lives. It was a condition we'd set, prompted by an infantile desire to preserve some imaginary idea of freedom, a concession that, although we never actually demanded it from each other or had any deeper need for it, seemed important to us back then. It was an aggressive reaction to our youth, in which we—perhaps Erica more so than I—had had little opportunity to nurture our own sense of freedom. We clung to it, in ways that seem frantic to me now. This condition is what held me back from the giving and accepting that comes with a deeper friendship. Our attempt not to meddle in each other's lives made that first year of living together a tour de force, and a long exercise in self-discipline on my part. Due to the instability of Erica's nature, there was no regularity in our household to speak of. Nevertheless, a steady routine emerged, one that we could stick to without feeling encumbered by it. We didn't talk about it, our life together just developed naturally.

I persuaded the landlord to knock down a wall so that Erica would get the alcove that connected our two rooms. My bed was pushed up against the sliding doors, and although they were always closed, we could still have late-night conversations before falling asleep, she in her bed in the alcove and me in mine behind the doors.

I'd closed those doors before we even signed the rental agreement. We were visiting the apartment for a third time just to make sure we'd made the right choice. Renting an apartment and all of the responsibilities that come with it brought me a lot of anxiety, which mostly hit me at night. But I didn't let it show. That Sunday afternoon, I stood in the back room and Erica in the alcove.

"Are you sure you want the front room, Erica?"

She nodded enthusiastically. "I'd rather have to hear cars and street noise than that," she said pointing to the balcony doors, which opened to the backsides of the houses on the street behind us. "Fishwives and domestic disputes—I've had enough of that to last a lifetime."

I didn't understand what she meant. The house where Erica and her mother lived with the General was on upscale Minervalaan. But I let it drop.

"Let's just tear down that wall, and then you can have the alcove. Otherwise your half is too small, my room is bigger. You can use the extra space for your bed and maybe a little table . . ."

"'Oh let's just tear down that wall,'" she mimicked. "You think the landlord is crazy?"

"I'll handle it," I said, suddenly feeling quite sure of myself. "And otherwise, we'll pay for it ourselves."

She gave me a probing look. "You know I don't have any money, don't you? But if you're so sure that the landlord . . ."

"So it's a deal?" I asked. "We'll sign?"

She nodded slowly without enthusiasm and without taking her eyes off me. For a moment of reprieve, I walked to the back of the house and closed the balcony doors. Then, with a knowing glance in Erica's direction—which elicited no reaction from her whatsoever—I closed the sliding doors in the middle of the room as well. This gesture was meant to symbolize our agreement to let each other be free. But in that moment, I didn't quite know how to put it into words.

Our decision, which we celebrated afterward with a cup of coffee at a cafeteria, was just a postlude. Erica hardly said a word; we drank our coffee and went our separate ways. The next morning, she called me from the newspaper.

"When are you going to sign?"

"During my lunch break."

"Don't forget about that wall!"

In the weeks that followed, Erica was enthusiastic. She ignored all the minor setbacks that come with moving into a new place with a stubborn sense of optimism. She let me clear the obstacles. The fact that I'd gotten the landlord's permission to tear down the wall had apparently convinced her of my capacities in such matters. I didn't tell her that in exchange I'd had to sign a two-year lease.

"Just take care of it," she'd say whenever I brought up topics like wallpaper, rugs, or hot water installations.

Propelled by her confidence in me, I found the courage to take on other endeavors that, under different circumstances, I would've never dared to try, I even went into debt. Erica was fully absorbed in furnishing her room. She was incredibly handy with tools. I'd never met a woman who was so good at carpentry. Her short, sturdy fingers were so skilled with a hammer and nails that within two weeks she had a primitively furnished room to move into. She didn't have any money for household furnishings, but she'd find things on the street and drag them home to the Prinsengracht.

In the evenings, she would transform them into useable pieces of furniture. Whenever I went back to my boardinghouse around midnight—I spent those weeks visiting the new apartment in the evening like a cat getting to know its new home—the light in her room was still on. I'd leave Erica bent over her work with a knee on the wood and a saw in her steady hand, a straight lock of hair hanging over her eyes, her sports blouse dark with sweat. The sound of her sawing and pounding echoed down the canal.

The next evening, when I asked her how late she'd stayed up working, she'd reply nonchalantly, "Until four o'clock or so, I think. The sun was starting to come up. It's quiet on the canal at night, so that's good to know." Or: "I just slept here," she'd say, pointing to a chair she'd just reupholstered. "It wasn't worth going home anymore. It sits great, nice and cushy."

Apparently, she was used to burning the midnight oil, and I couldn't help but wonder if she was going to keep me up all night. I needed eight hours of undisturbed sleep.

When it came time to transfer my things to the new apartment, she unexpectedly took charge. My plans to hire movers were immediately dismissed.

"What a waste of money!" she said.

"But how, then?" I asked, intimidated by the tone of her voice, which suddenly made my moving plans seem extravagant.

"We'll figure it out."

She didn't tell me about her plans until the day before, when I hesitantly reminded her of her responsibility.

"Pa's warehouse guy is coming by tomorrow afternoon at five-thirty with a pushcart. Make sure you're ready."

It was the first time she'd ever mentioned "Pa." Until then, I'd assumed that her father was dead and that her Ma was a widow who'd been forced to find other means of subsistence. The fact that Erica hadn't said anything about it had led me to draw what seemed to be a logical conclusion, but one that was, in fact, completely false. Even then, she didn't elaborate on the subject, and I didn't dare probe her any further.

I'll never forget that first evening in our new apartment. Pa's warehouse guy had to make two trips between my boarding-house and the new place. On the first trip, his cart was already half full with Erica's stuff, which he had picked up from the General's house. When he finally left, after receiving Erica's "regards to Pa" and five guilders from me, we set to work. We were busy unpacking until eleven o'clock, and I remember making a lot of trips up and down the hallway, because, even then, the sliding doors remained shut. Afterward, we went out for coffee and goofed around a bit at a neighborhood bar. It wasn't until we came home and I was ready to go to bed that I had a look at the fruits of Erica's labor. All of a sudden, I realized what had been vaguely bothering me during the move. Something was missing, but in all the chaos I hadn't thought much about it. That morning, when I saw Erica's possessions on the cart—a few boxes, a suitcase, a chair, and a typewriter—I felt a bit sorry for her, but the thought of all the furniture she'd made for her new room put my mind at ease. Her room had struck me as a bit bare, but I figured it was just the move. She just needed some time to unpack and establish a sense of order. But when we finally said goodnight, I found myself standing in her doorway and watching her unroll a bundle of blankets on the floor—then I knew.

"Erica, where's your bed? You forgot your bed!"

She stood up and looked at me. A shy, crooked smile stretched across her face.

"I sleep on the ground," she said.

Despite that smile, her voice was grave and decisive. But I forced myself to press further.

"But you can't . . .That's ridiculous . . ."

"Oh, I can sleep anywhere," she interjected, and after seeing the look on my face, she added reassuringly, "I'll buy a second-hand bed one of these days, don't worry."

I blamed myself for my thoughtlessness, for the feeling of indignation I couldn't quite place. "Why didn't you say anything?" I asked. "I could have lent you the money . . ."

She sat down on the pile of blankets and wrapped her arms around her knees. Then she burst into laughter. "Haven't you ever slept on the floor? What if there was a fire or a flood, and you had to flee your home . . ."

"Erica, cut it out . . ." I didn't know what to say. This was something I couldn't take lightly even if I'd wanted to. I couldn't joke with her about this. But she'd already stopped laughing. She turned and stared out the window for a few minutes. The room was suddenly so quiet that I could hear the clock ticking in my room behind the doors.

"Ma didn't want to give me the bed," she said, gazing out the window at the dark silhouettes of the trees on the moonlit canal.

"It must have belonged to the General," I remember joking, a feeble attempt to help her. In fact, the entire unpleasant episode is forever engraved in my memory.

Erica shrugged.

"Well . . . sweet dreams . . ." I said.

"You too."

"Our first night . . ." What was I supposed to say?

"Yes."

I lay awake for hours. It was quiet in that canal house, but I couldn't sleep.

Erica slept on the ground, wrapped in her cocoon of blankets, for at least six weeks. For her birthday that October, I gave her a bed as a present. I hadn't brought up the issue since that first night. Erica's attitude made it impossible. There were countless times when I wanted to say something but couldn't find the words. Before we went to sleep, at work, on my way home—the fact that I still hadn't said anything about it seemed ridiculous. But whenever I was with her, I just couldn't find a casual way of asking: "So, about the bed—should we just go out and get one tomorrow?" On numerous occasions, I found myself peering into furniture store windows, and one time, I even went inside to ask about prices and then made up an excuse about why I had to leave again. When the bed was delivered early in the morning on her birthday (the whole adventure had required stealthy planning and cost me numerous headaches) Erica just muttered, "Thanks." Then, all of a sudden, she hurled herself onto the bed, bounced up and down a few times and said: "It's just right, not too soft."

It was on that birthday that I met Ma. Erica had announced the visit without any jokes or commentary. When the doorbell rang, she went down to answer it, and the stairwell filled with commotion: exclamations, laughter, exaggerated huffing and puffing, loud sighs—like a column of noise slowly traveling up the stairs. Then, when Ma finally reached the top, she repeated a more moderate version of the entire scene. "My goodness, what a climb, child, you're in the clouds up here. Hello young lady!" (A loud kiss). "Happy birthday! My, what a nice place you've got here. I'll get you a runner for those stairs. Where's your friend? Goodness, gracious! Happy, happy birthday, m'dear. Here, this is for you!"

I was in the kitchen making tea. I listened in vain for the sound of Erica's voice. Without a word, she steered her mother into her room and closed the door. I stood in the hallway, tea tray in hand, not sure what to do next.

Later, I found myself sitting across from Erica's mother, a robust woman with Erica's mouth and shoe-polish-black hair. I kept the conversation going, which didn't take a lot of effort. I found Ma (as I began calling her that afternoon) fascinating and hilarious. She was full of stories, eager to answer simple questions and showed interest in our lives. As usual, Erica was quiet.

After she'd retreated to her room and shut the door, which, after a moment's hesitation, I decided to just ignore, I assumed she was ashamed of her mother. But once again, I was wrong. She'd even smiled at Ma's coarse, boisterous humor. We'd exchanged looks several times, and there hadn't been a hint of embarrassment in her eyes. She even took her mother's hateful, mocking remarks about "your Pa" in stride. She just sat there on the ground calmly smoking a cigarette with her arms wrapped around her knees. I have to admit there were moments when even I couldn't help but feel embarrassed, when Ma's laughter became just a bit too exuberant, her anecdote a bit too far-fetched, her confession a bit too frank. I tried to catch Erica's gaze to see if she shared my feelings—to gauge how painful it was for her—but her face and posture remained completely passive. She doesn't care, I realized in awe. She was objective and amused—not at all bored by her mother's stories and jokes, which she must've heard hundreds of times. After

Ma had left (she was meeting the colonel—the "General," in Erica's parlance—for dinner in the city), I went to the kitchen to cook a nice meal for the two of us. But Erica stopped me. In her hand were five guilders. "A present from Ma," she said. "Come on, let's splurge."

We had dinner at Kempinsky's that night, but Erica barely touched her food. Later, I found myself reaching for my own wallet to pay off the rest of the bill. After two bottles of Bols, she'd kept right on ordering. I struggled to get her home and had to help her put on her pajamas. She leaned against me sleepily and kept saying I was a sweet bitch and kissing me on the neck. Despite her level of intoxication, she'd been able to carry on a rational conversation all the way back to our house. It was more of a monologue really, with Erica telling witty, entertaining stories of her job at the newspaper and funny descriptions of her coworkers.

That night, I lay awake thinking about the five guilders. The gift had been dug out of her mother's dowdy handbag on the street, boisterously carried up the stairs and delivered on the top step. "Here, this is for you!" I didn't know who to feel sorry for: the mother or the daughter. It brought back memories of my birthdays back home, the yellow daisies on my chair and around my fork and knife at the breakfast table, elegantly wrapped presents around my plate, the cake with candles—one for every five years as I got older, my father's quiet delight, it all came flooding back. At breakfast the next day, Erica joked about the bed.

"Now that I have one, I can't sleep!" she said.

"Didn't the Bols help?" I asked.

"Yes, you would think. I was really putting 'em back, huh?"

"You could say that."

She shook her head. "See? It must've been the bed. And you know what occurred to me?" She gave me a look of comical despair, and I sensed an attempt to make amends for something.

"You're going to have to buy me bedsheets and pillowcases now, too."

"Sounds like a nice present for Sinterklaas," I said, embarrassed to once again be playing her benefactor.

"No need," she replied, "Pa gave me ten guilders. You buy them, I don't know the first thing about linens."

Later, before she left for the newspaper, she gave me the money.

"What a waste," she said, and on her way down the stairs, she shouted up, "Bea . . . I should have used the money to buy a *dress*!" She seemed to find this funny and walked out the door laughing.

For the most part, those early days with Erica were a mystery to me. But every now and then, she'd get to talking. For no reason at all, she'd suddenly launch into a story about her youth, which gave me some peace of mind about the problems that were troubling me.

Her stories were always depressing, tragic, but she didn't see them that way, or so I thought back then—most of the time they made me laugh. But then I'd have trouble sleeping. From her experiences came certain phrases and expressions that we'd use among ourselves, which gave us a feeling of intimacy and solidarity. We repeated Pa's lamentations to Ma, "You'll be dancing on my grave," and Ma's catchphrases like, "We're going to Grandma's!" which she used to shout from the attic window whenever Pa disappeared into the bar across the street.

There'd come a time when Erica wouldn't be able to see the humor in all this anymore, but that wasn't until much later.

2

WIES GREETED THE NEWS of our companionship with enthusiasm. She assigned herself the role of deus ex machina and made a big fuss about it. In her mind, we were two lonely wanderers who, thanks to her talent for bringing people together, had found salvation in each other. The fact that the hand of providence had played a greater role in it than anything—after all, my visit to Wies's house that summer evening was completely unplanned—escaped her entirely, and I didn't want to deny her the satisfaction. Naturally, I shared my feelings—or I should say my lack of feelings—for Wies with Erica, though somewhat hesitantly.

"But I'll probably have to go see her again at some point," I concluded.

"Why would you?" Erica replied.

"She means well, and she took good care of me when I was sick."

"So what? And really, she did all that for herself. People like Wies are kind and caring for their own satisfaction."

With those words, not only had she summed up Wies's character, she also (and much to the relief of my guilty conscience) shed some light on my visits to Wies's house.

As to why Erica occasionally visited Wies herself, I had no idea, and I didn't ask. All she told me was that Wies used to work in the archives at the newspaper. But I was sure that, for some reason, she actually liked Wies. Erica was not someone who did other people favors to get them to like her. She had no problem making enemies. I couldn't figure out what kind of people she liked, at least not in that first year. I didn't see many people in those days and had very few visitors. I avoided my old friends because I was still nursing an open wound and certain encounters were inevitably painful. Whenever I did introduce Erica to people, she was friendly but reserved. Only after about six months or so (I don't remember exactly when it started) did she start speaking her mind about my friends. Most of the time, her criticism was, even for her—and from an objective stand-point really—unreasonably harsh. This surprised me because up to that point, the only Erica I knew was tolerant by nature and deep down quite warm.

Out of curiosity, I accompanied her on a visit to Wies's house. I wanted to find out once and for all what attracted her to such a clingy creature whom I felt so indifferent toward, to someone I found so incredibly irritating but was still too weak to shake.

When I told her I wanted to go with her, Erica raised her eyebrows in surprise but then replied, "How nice." She slipped her arm through mine and insisted that we go on foot. Wies lived all the way on the south side of Amsterdam, but Erica said she wanted to enjoy the fall evening. We spoke very little. I was tired after a busy day at the office. Erica, who had surely had a hectic day at the paper as well, was not. But she was quiet. She didn't say a word until we walked by Café Parkzicht, and she told me that her boss sat there at the same table every night. All of a sudden, her quietness exploded into a flurry of excitement, which startled me a bit. She dragged me across the street and ordered me to—without attracting any attention—take a peek inside.

"Look, there on the left, you can see him sitting by the window. Tall and blond with glasses." I didn't see anyone and said so loudly. With the same unbridled excitement, she pulled me back across the street to the entrance of the park. As we crossed the road, she kept looking back over her shoulder in a way that was not at all inconspicuous. She was acting like a schoolgirl; I was completely taken aback by her behavior. She'd hardly ever mentioned her boss and talked about him much less than she did about her other co-workers. Later as I was trying to piece together everything that happened in my mind, I kept coming back to that evening.

"We're going through the park, aren't we?" she asked unnecessarily.

"Yes, of course," I replied and went on to say how much I loved the smell of wet, rotting leaves, how it reminded me of my childhood in The Hague and riding my bicycle along the edge of the woods on my way home from school, but I was still thinking about what had just happened. It had already occurred to me on occasion that Erica avoided the topic of men. Her excitement that evening was out of character. But what on earth did she talk about with Wies then? Wies, as I knew from my weeks in the hospital with her, was constantly steering the conversation back to men. If you asked me, it was one of her worst qualities and one of the things I appreciated most about Erica.

We walked slowly through the park, which was full of other people who, like us, were bidding farewell to summer and trying to find comfort in the arrival of fall. I couldn't help but wonder whether this really was the best season of the year, when things die and decay, making room for new growth in the spring. Whenever the season forces itself upon me as strongly as it did that day, it has a way of making me feel sentimental, melancholic even. I was so moved by the memory of those daily bike rides home from school, of my father waiting for me with tea, that I couldn't say much. But still, I wanted to help Erica by making small talk—she must have known that she'd behaved strangely, I thought, though she didn't seem the least bit embarrassed. We strolled leisurely through the park toward the exit. All around us, the leaves were letting go of their tired branches and slowly falling to the ground. We shuffled our feet across the withered carpet, a more moderate version of the game from childhood.

When we got to Wies's house, Erica plopped right down on the couch. She propped a pillow under her head and lay there, completely at home, exactly as I'd found her the first time we met. Wies was thrilled. She did everything she could to make us comfortable, which created an atmosphere of uneasiness that kept me on the edge of my seat. ("No, no, I'm fine here, Wies, really. Yes, tea is fine. No, nothing else for me. No, it's not too hot in here. I don't feel a draft at all. No, thank you, I'd really rather sit in this chair.") Erica watched in silence and didn't take her eyes off Wies.

"What do you think of my dress, Erica?" Wies asked, and I noticed with irritation how the girl who wore sports blouses and wool socks, whom I'd never heard utter a serious word about clothes or fashion, called the ensemble "darling." She gushed over the Chinese collar and asked Wies if she had done something different with her hair. Did she get a perm? How much did it cost? The conversation that evening exceeded all limits, I thought. Inane chatter about clothes, men, Wies's stubborn cleaning lady, and, of course, Huib, Wies's ex-husband, whom I'd come to know intimately from all her stories in the hospital, as if I had witnessed him twirling around in front of the mirror in his underwear every night myself. I was annoyed, and at the same time bothered by how annoyed I was because, as far as I could tell, there was no reason for a deeper or more interesting conversation. But no matter how hard I tried to fit in, I just couldn't, which made me feel self-conscious and awkwardly reserved. What a snob I am, I thought.

We took the tram home and discussed our plans for the next day, which was a Sunday. Erica was completely herself again. We decided to take the steam tram to the coast and go for a walk in the dunes. But the next morning, Erica wouldn't get out of bed. She said she was tired and asked to be left alone. She told me to go about my day and not worry about her.

This started happening more often. She spent entire Sundays in bed. If I stayed home, I'd hear her stumble into the kitchen or the bathroom a couple of times, but otherwise the house would be completely silent. During the week, she slept very little. Often, she'd stay up reading late into the night or she'd write—what she was writing, or about whom, I had no idea. But all my worries that she'd keep me up at night turned out to be for nothing. She was always quiet. The only reason I even knew she stayed up all night was the vertical strip of light between the sliding doors. That she slept through an entire Sunday every once in a while seemed understandable to me, and the logic behind her behavior was somewhat comical. I always tried to be as quiet as possible, though she'd never asked me to do so.

I guess you could say I found the fact that Erica spent entire days in bed amusing that first year; later, however, I began to attach a certain significance to them and could predict when she was going to disappear under the covers.

There were so many times when I thought I'd finally figured her out, but looking back on it later, I could only smile disparagingly—a little sadly even—at my own self-proclaimed "insight." Even now, with my broader understanding of humanity, I wonder whether what I took to be a tree growing off in the distance wasn't in fact a lifeless trunk, its own leaves strangled by the vines growing up around it.

Shortly before Christmas, Erica inherited three thousand guilders—or rather Ma had received the money as an inheritance from a childless uncle and given it all to Erica. She went to visit her at the newspaper and shoved the envelope of cash into her hands. As soon as I heard Erica coming up the stairs, I knew something out of the ordinary had happened. She was singing a silly tune from her vast repertoire of old Dutch folk songs—to my great amusement she knew them all by heart. Whether the song had two verses or ten, Erica could sing every word. And they were always twice as entertaining when she sang them. She tapped the envelope against the wall as she made her way up the stairs, clip-clop, clip-clop, ". . . *and no, no, we're not going home . . .*" I could tell right away she'd been drinking. She tossed the envelope in my direction, sank down in a kitchen chair, and, with her head on the table, began laughing loudly.

"Ma, the benefactor!" she said finally, wiping tears from her eyes. "Three thousand guilders for Erica!"

Exactly what Ma had said, she didn't say. Erica walked out of the kitchen with the envelope pinched between her thumb and forefinger like a rag, and I drained the potatoes. It wasn't until a few minutes later that I became aware of the rigid smile on my face.

Erica didn't come back to eat until I was peeling an apple for my dessert. She scooped herself a heaping portion of sauerkraut and ate with gusto. Every now and then, I saw her shake her head ever so slightly and suppress another fit of laughter. I peeled her a tangerine and carefully placed the pieces around the edge of her plate. As I did, she suddenly looked at me and her eyes filled with tears. "Bea, Bea," she said, and using Grandma's expression declared: "Life's just full of surprises."

"Let's go to the movies," she said, "or how about the theater? I'm rich! What time is it? We can just make it."

The mad dash to get cleaned up and dressed came as a relief to me. We saw some kind of American comedy and drank coffee at intermission. On the way home, Erica suddenly dropped my arm. "I'm going to walk on a bit," she said and turned down a side street. She didn't come home until the next morning.

The money disappeared like snow in the sun. We had an English Christmas that year with a tree and presents—a wristwatch and a new radio for me. Erica bought herself expensive dresses and shoes, which she never wore, piles of books, a gramophone, and more records than we had room for in the house. Quartets and piano concerts, Greta Keller and *The Threepenny Opera* reverberated across our entire floor all evening long. At Erica's insistence, we ate out in restaurants, went to concerts, and didn't miss a single premier at the theater.

She was in a feverish hurry to get rid of that money. At first, I was against all the luxury because I didn't have the means to contribute, but soon enough I was letting myself be treated without protest. It was as if she needed to be rid of the money as quickly as possible, I thought. And if that was her goal, I wasn't going to try and stop her. Don't judge, for the love of God, don't judge! That was one of my major convictions in those days. Live together, but don't try to censure each other. Hopefully, it would all blow over soon. I couldn't stand her feverishness, her inflated sense of happiness.

On New Year's Eve, our house was suddenly full of people. Erica's colleagues came stomping up the stairs—overgrown boys who masked their insecurity with a pompous air. They limited themselves to ready-made phrases recited in a snob- bish accent with raised eyebrows: a helpless "Right, right" or a friendly "Oh really? I wasn't aware of that!" Most were aging bachelors, weighed down by years of disappointment in journalism and the endless race for the last paragraph. The type of men who know everything and speak in a condescending tone ("I'm tellin' you, sweetheart, time sure does fly") and they proved extremely helpful when it came to preparing the cold supper. I counted two couples: one that seemed mildly amused by our little ladies' apartment, and the other consisting of a loud old gentleman, who had clearly just escaped a boring family get-together, and his unwilling wife. She was wearing an enormous cameo on her blouse and an ivory-bead necklace that hung down to her waist, and by her second glass of warm wine, she'd already started complaining about her fate as the wife of a journalist. And there was a nice girl, secretary to "the boss," who, as the evening progressed, was burdened with all kinds of candid messages to pass on to her employer. I hadn't invited anyone. It was Erica's evening, and I was still avoiding my friends.

"I'm going to give a little soirée." Erica had announced two evenings prior. How she ever found all these people to come at the last minute was a mystery to me, but after having spoken to all the guests within the first fifteen minutes, I realized that what she was really doing was providing the lonely and least popular with an opportunity to celebrate the New Year. It was the type of evening where you find yourself cleaning ashtrays and sticky glasses at the end of the night and wondering what the point of it was—why you even bothered having a party in the first place. And how self-conscious it all makes you feel, as if you can never live up to people's expectations. The guests milled around desperately searching for something, anything they could latch on to, and if that didn't work, if a conversation didn't offer the satisfaction they were looking for, they'd circulate through the small apartment, from Erica's room to my room, and end up at the kitchen table trying to make small talk with me as I busied myself with the refreshments. It was the kind of evening where the most idiotic banalities were flung around with bravado in the hope that they might attract attention and, in doing so, make up for the awkwardness of it all, where even the more profound observations shriveled against the ceiling like balloons slipped from children's hands. At first, Erica didn't quite know what to do with herself in this situation she'd created. I'd picked up on the shyness of her smile, the constant smoking and the restless, aimless way she drifted from one group to the other; all of this compelled me to try to put her guests at ease. I left no glass unfilled, brought the sandwiches and meat pastries out a whole hour earlier than planned and chatted incessantly. By midnight, however, Erica had had so much to drink that she didn't even notice the forced atmosphere and barely concealed boredom. I know for a fact that she considered the entire soirée a smashing success, and her toast to the new year was candid and long. Around two o'clock in the morning, the bottom of the punchbowl was in sight, and I was running out of stamina. I silently prayed that someone would stand up to leave and suddenly everyone would notice the time. But just then, the doorbell rang.

"Who could that be?" someone shouted, and then, "More guests!"

"Now the party can start!" shouted one of the blowhards hopefully.

Erica went to open the door and came back, sober and pale, with her boss. I'd never met him, I'd only ever heard about him in the vaguest terms, but I knew it was him the second he walked in the door. The mood changed instantly. Some of the guests immediately tried to make a good impression, while others retreated back into their shells. Ultimately, everyone ended up in my bedroom, where the boss had taken a seat on the couch. The bolder ones among them gathered around him in chairs and on the ground, while the shyer ones hovered around the balcony and the open door to the hallway. I went to the kitchen to make more sandwiches and poured the last bit of punch into a glass. When I returned to my room and offered the boss some refreshments, I noticed that Erica was gone. I found her in her room frantically cleaning. She emptied the ashtrays out the window facing the canal, fluffed the pillows and straightened the chairs. She didn't see me, and

I tiptoed back out of the room. By then, there was an animated conversation going on in my room, and I tried to find a place in the circle. The boss was clearly enjoying all the attention. He reminded me of a father who was just checking in to see what the kids were up to, as if the teenagers had been allowed to have a little party in the living room while the parents tried to make themselves as comfortable as possible upstairs, mother stretched out on the bed with a book and a cup of tea on the nightstand and father hunched over his paperwork at the vanity. After a few outbursts of laughter downstairs and a few knowing glances at each other, they decided that dad would just go down—amiably and in a spirit of camaraderie, of course—and have a look. I have to admit the boss irritated me. He was just *so* interested in what everyone had to say. He led the conversation with such artificial tact and so many nods of understanding that I was tempted to make a belittling comment or two just to cut him down to size.

The conversation was about politics: the state, the individual versus the state and the masses. It was a fairly common topic in those days given the situations in Spain and Germany. The boss's ideas and conclusions didn't sit well with me. I waited in vain for someone to stand up for the individual, but nobody in the room seemed to feel the urge to protest. After a half-hour, I went to check on Erica—she'd never come out to join the group. Her door was open, the room had been cleaned (in a very Erica-like fashion), but she wasn't there. I checked the shower, the bathroom, the kitchen (I even opened the door to the balcony), but she was nowhere to be found, and I realized with shock that she'd just left. I sat on her bed waiting for her to come home. Maybe she'd just gone out for some fresh air or to buy cigarettes at the neighborhood bar that was open all night. Every now and then I'd get up, go to my room, empty a few ashtrays, collect the plates and glasses carelessly cast aside and take them into the kitchen. Then I'd go back to Erica's room and lean out the window over the canal, hoping that one of the late-night partygoers in the distance would be her. But she didn't come home, and when her party guests were finally getting ready to leave, I closed the door to her bedroom and told them in a hushed tone that Erica had gone to bed with a splitting headache. I saw everyone out and prayed that they wouldn't run into Erica on the street. But she never turned up. I boiled some water and did the dishes, tidied up the house, swept the living room, tended to the stove, and when I finally crawled into bed completely exhausted as the sun was coming up, there wasn't a trace of the party left in the house. Even the cigarette smoke had been whisked out the window and into the clear, cold night.

I lay shivering under the covers. It was suddenly so cold in the apartment. Why had Erica left? Vague suspicions and theories ran through my mind, and I kept coming back to that pale look on her face when she walked in the room with her boss, and how she'd behaved a few months earlier on the way to Wies's house when she dragged me across the street. Then my thoughts turned to Wies. Why hadn't Erica invited her? Was she maybe spending the night at her house? But then why would she, I wondered resentfully. I sprang out of bed and went to the kitchen to warm up some milk. As I lay against the pillows sipping my bedtime drink, I heard Erica's keys in the door. I quickly switched off the light, crawled back under the covers and listened to her sneak up the stairs.

3

I PROMISED MYSELF that I wouldn't say anything to Erica about her strange behavior, and to be honest, I didn't even have a chance because Ma showed up first thing in the morning to wish us a happy new year and talked nonstop. The General had invited some friends over to ring in the new year, and Ma needed a full hour to express her outrage over the way they had treated her.

"They completely ignored me," she lamented. "I was only there to make dinner! Nothing but a maid!"

As soon as she left, Erica retreated into her room and didn't come out again. That afternoon, I went to visit my family and had dinner in the city. The New Year's Eve party wasn't mentioned again. A few days later, Erica presented me with a savings account book in her name and asked me to keep watch over her inheritance, that is, the five hundred guilders that was left of it.

"Why don't you do it yourself?" I asked, not entirely thrilled with the role of treasurer being tossed in my lap.

She ignored my question. "More money's coming," she said nonchalantly. "There are a few people who owe me."

Less than a week later, she came to ask for fifty guilders.

"You mean you want your bankbook back?" I asked, opening the desk drawer I'd stashed it in. "Listen, Erica. I don't feel comfortable with this arrangement. It's ridiculous for me to be keeping tabs on your money, for you to have to ask me every time you need some. You need to manage the bankbook yourself."

She stubbornly refused. Her face turned bright red, but she didn't explain her reasoning. That same day, I found the book back on my desk. We went back to living the simple life we'd had before Erica became rich and her balance remained untouched. The fact that we suddenly had to watch every cent felt strange. Erica seemed to find the whole thing funny; she made jokes about us having seven meager years ahead of us. And in truth, in contrast to the sober existence our incomes actually afforded, that brief period of opulence felt much longer than the few weeks it had lasted. We didn't have much, but we lived fairly well. Erica was still stuck paying off her debt to Ma. Her full salary would have afforded her a slightly more comfortable lifestyle, but just like before, she could only deposit a limited amount in our household fund. And since she refused to let me put any extra money into our pot in the kitchen cupboard, I spent less than my own income allowed. I concluded that she hadn't used her inheritance to pay back her debt to Ma for her time volunteering at the local newspaper. I didn't understand why, but I suspected it had something to do with the other bizarre aspects of her history. Erica's strange behavior the day she'd received the money and the fact that her garrulous mother never said a word about it again on any of her later visits were proof that the whole thing was an epilogue to a family drama I knew nothing about.

It was a cozy winter, and we enjoyed ourselves. Gradually, I started renewing old ties. I invited friends over for dinner and went out more often. My attempts to bring Erica into the circle were only partially successful. She kept her distance, and after a while, when she started expressing her criticism and aversion, I stopped trying. To keep the balance, I even insisted on inviting Wies, but Erica wasn't interested. Wies never came to our house, and I could only wonder whether Erica saw her regularly. Still, Erica and I spent a lot of time together, and she seemed to enjoy it. Many evenings were spent reading together in my room. We also had occasional bursts of activity, when we'd suddenly take up leatherwork or something and spend weeks fiddling around with awls and knives, making all kinds of things—some more useful than others. Then we'd decide to study graphology or sign up for fencing lessons. None of it lasted very long. Erica would come up with the idea, but after a short bout of enthusiasm, she'd had enough. And since I'd let myself be swept up in her excitement and my own dedication was based solely on her ambition, my interest would quickly wane as well. The bursts of activity were signs of Erica's restlessness, excuses to avoid her own inner turmoil, activities she imposed on herself so that she would never get around to the things she actually wanted to do. I sensed it already back then, but I couldn't put my finger on it. These thoughts were nothing more than vague ideas spinning around in my head that I couldn't pin down.

"What shall we do, Erica?" I'd ask.

"What do you mean?" she'd say. "Nothing. We don't have to do anything, do we? Why are you always nagging me about what to do?"

At the same time, however, she had absolutely no idea what to do with herself. She'd pick up a book, flip through it, pick up another, offer to make tea but then not do it, eat an apple, lie on the couch, write, stand in front of the window for half an hour, go in the kitchen, tear up whatever it was she'd written, and then ask: "Want to go to the movies?"

I didn't understand why her work didn't already keep her busy enough. Journalism was an interesting profession, after all, and I always thought that journalists and reporters spent their entire evenings out on assignments or gathering news.

When I asked Erica about this, her response was sarcastic. Oh sure, it was a romantic profession, she just hadn't gotten to the romantic part yet. In the foreign news department, the most prized skills were cutting and pasting, and she was so handy with scissors and glue that they just couldn't spare her.

"Not to mention your knowledge of foreign languages," I said encouragingly.

She shrugged.

"What good is that?" she said. "It's just an office job, Bea. One day, I hope to write about art. That's my goal—the Art and Literature department, but . . ." She finished the sentence with a disheartened gesture. "I'm not a careerist," she added. "Besides, I'm only twenty-one."

She was disappointed with her job, her profession, and I was annoyed by the short-sightedness of her employers, who underestimated her potential.

But none of those things were the source of her restlessness, that I knew. It was something deeper inside her, something to do with her actual being, though she could have certainly found sublimation in her work for what was troubling her emotionally.

Once, following a hunch, I asked her if she was in love. She looked at me in shock: "What makes you think that? Me? In love?" The bitter lines on the sides of her mouth deepened into dark trenches. Then, as if struck by sudden inspiration, she said, "Maybe I *am* in love, God knows."

I could tell the topic intrigued her, so I pressed a bit further: "Your boss, perhaps?"

She laughed out loud. "What? You think I'm in love with *him*?"

I realized then how childish and naïve the question was and started to laugh in spite of myself. "I guess you're the only one who can answer that question," I said.

"Yeah, one would assume so!"

She burst out laughing again, and I, sensing her sarcasm, crawled back into my shell.

"What did you think of him?" she asked in an attempt at seriousness, which was undoubtedly intended to put me at ease so I'd feel forced to confide in her. His name hadn't come up since the New Year's Eve party, and the question was painful. She must've sensed my hesitation or seen it in my face, because she cut me off by saying that he was a very special person.

"That could be," I replied vaguely.

"He's very well informed," she said almost apologetically. "I have lunch with him sometimes," she added, and suddenly, as if the confession had been one step too far, she scowled at me, said I asked the strangest questions, and left the room. It was up to me to draw my own conclusion, but I didn't know what to make of the whole thing. I thought about it a lot, recalling Erica's teenage behavior during our walk that fall, but I didn't get much further than that. For some inexplicable reason, I just couldn't see Erica with her boss, and since I wouldn't allow myself to meddle in Erica's personal affairs—not even in my mind—I brushed the whole thing off. The subject of men didn't come up again until a few weeks before Easter, when I met Bas. He was the manager of our Rotterdam branch and visited our office regularly to meet with my boss, who was on doctor's orders to take it easy and limit his work to Amsterdam.

It was with Bas that I had my first real relationship. I'd had two other boyfriends before him, and although I don't really count them anymore, I still remember my total surrender—and my misery after our separation. They were short, intense affairs, both of which ended in depression, followed by temporary isolation to rediscover my sense of self-worth. Here in America, I've had my share of adventures, but nothing has ever become of them. In my life, men have always been like shadows waiting in the wings. There was never room for them on stage because Erica held the spotlight.

Women my age are often asked in moments of confidence why they never married, and they usually answer that they never wanted to or that they just never found the right guy. I give both answers. Though secretly I wonder whether my relationship with Bas had met all the conditions for a happy marriage. But such contemplations are unproductive at best.

I already knew from Bas's correspondence with my boss that he was a kind, level-headed man. You can tell a lot about a person by the way they write business letters. In addition to the qualities I found attractive in him, he also matched the physical image I'd constructed. Okay, he was a bit shorter than I'd imagined, but still stocky enough to instill trust. He'd gone gray quite young, but he still had a youthful face and the healthy complexion of a man without major conflicts in his life. I liked his broad, well-formed hands and fantastic smile.

Maybe I dissected his physical attributes one by one so I could size them up against my own. I've never seen any reason to boast about my own appearance. Even back then, I was what men called drab. I'd always been pale and skinny, my coarse hair a dull shade of blond, and I had no interest in or talent for fashion. But I had good hands and—as Erica had once pointed out—pretty teeth.

Bas reminded me of my father, and I immediately felt so safe with him when he took me out for lunch that I invited him home with me that same evening.

He ended up staying the night. It amazes me how easily I used to let myself be seduced into extreme intimacies. I shared my bed with men whose bodies were as strange to me as their physiognomy. The second time I'd recognize their facial expressions and feel incredibly embarrassed about the memory of the first time. After all, our first night together couldn't have been much different? So, what was the point of those first few nights? But maybe I was afraid that after having been friends, I wouldn't be able to enter into a physical relationship. Perhaps I found it easier after a few drinks. After an evening of wandering hands, I'd be half-numb with exhaustion and end up giving in blindly. The pattern was always the same.

Still, it wasn't until the morning, after listening carefully for any sound behind the sliding doors, that I gave him—passively and because I felt more or less obliged to—the satisfaction he'd been waiting for all night. But Bas was patient, and he stayed patient all the nights we shared my bed.

As I look back on the whole episode, it's clearer to me how vague feelings of guilt had already contaminated much of the happiness I would have otherwise drawn from the new relationship. But it's precisely because of the ambivalence of my emotions, which manifested themselves in the form of unmotivated apologies, concessions, and a constant feeling of guilt, that I'll never forget what happened on Easter Monday. Bas had been there since Good Friday, and I insisted that Erica join us for Easter weekend. Even when Bas surprised me with two tickets to the theater, which he had purchased on his way over from the station, my first question was, "What about Erica?" I ignored the look of surprise on his face, his objections, and asked if he wouldn't mind picking up a third ticket on Saturday morning. Since I absolutely insisted that we all sit together, he had to trade in our tickets for three seats that weren't nearly as good. Of course, the whole thing bothered me. I told myself I was stuck in the middle because I wasn't able to see how unreasonable I was being. Erica belonged with us. I wasn't going to just leave her to her own devices for the entire holiday weekend. The fact that Bas refused to accept this, even after my clear arguments, seemed unfair to me. At the same time, Erica's attitude about it all surprised me. When I announced that the three of us were going to the theater together, she smiled and said "good" or "nice" or something, I don't remember exactly. I had expected her to protest, to reluctantly give in out of politeness, at which I was prepared to reassure her that she belonged with us.

But of course, she again reacted differently than I'd expected and nothing more was said about it. Afterward, I tried to make it up to Bas. That indefinable feeling of embarrassment weighed on me more heavily than ever that weekend, and I bent over backward for Bas. I remember how on Easter morning I woke up early and cleaned my room on tiptoe before he woke up. I brought him breakfast in bed, forced him to stay there so I could place the cheerful breakfast tray on his lap even though he would've preferred to get up and had breakfast in the kitchen.

"Just relax and stay in bed," I protested, "it's all taken care of!" Erica was in the kitchen in her pajamas making coffee, strong coffee—she couldn't make it through the day without it—and started singing, "*Mother, oh how I need you . . .*" one of those old Dutch tunes she knew so well.

In all those months of living together, I'd never gotten angry with her, never lost my patience or resisted any of her antics, but all of a sudden, I felt an anger boiling up inside me. My heart was pounding, my hands were shaking, I didn't know what I was doing or what I should do. I walked to the counter in a confused haze.

"Erica," I hissed, "Erica, stop, Erica, give me some peace." She just kept singing, every single word of the song, two verses. This is unbearable, I thought suddenly. I've got to get out of here, I have to get away from her, this is no life for me, I can't stand her anymore.

Why the sudden change? Where was this extreme aversion to Erica coming from? I can't remember whether it occurred to me at that moment that the source of both my guilt and sudden rage was the night before. The realization probably came later, brought by the kaleidoscope of time. That night, I'd been unable to give myself to Bas, even though I'd gotten good at overcoming my reluctance by then. I just couldn't get over my embarrassment at the thought of Erica listening to us on the other side of the door. Bas's quiet surprise, followed by his tactful questions, led to a sleepless night, which was even more intolerable because I wasn't used to sharing my bed. Since I didn't want Bas to know I couldn't sleep, I just lay there motionless until morning. Now I wonder what was going through my head during those long, oppressive hours. Was I really so naïve that I only thought about what would happen the next day and not about the deeper conflict hiding behind my inexplicable inhibition? I don't know anymore. But I must have surprised myself, even more so because I'd felt a similar incapacity with one of my two previous lovers. If those relationships had been nothing but disappointment and heartache, it wasn't due to any impotency on my part. If anything, it was the opposite that had led to the breakup, and in both cases, I was left feeling powerless and needed time to cool down. The painful weeks that followed, during which I wondered why I was incapable of fascinating men, were forever engraved in my consciousness.

Only after she'd sung the last line of her drinking song did Erica acknowledge my irritation. She placed a loving hand on my neck and said soothingly: "Don't pay any attention to me, darling, I'm a bitch."

There was honest repentance in her voice, I couldn't help but notice a bit of triumph as well. What a child, I thought, appeased. She sang that song all the way through to the end. Now I know better. She was in a good mood all morning, and that afternoon, she went out.

"I'm going to go see Wies," she announced frankly, "and then to eat at Ma's. The General's out." She rolled her eyes to show how much she was looking forward to that dinner.

"I'll see you two at the theater."

That afternoon I repaid my debt to Bas, at least that's how it felt, and momentarily free, I even enjoyed our dinner at Dicker & Thys and the theater. Erica's mood had changed; she was friendly but preoccupied. Afterward, I walked with Bas to the station. When I got back to the apartment, Erica wasn't there, and I didn't hear her come home. Before I fell asleep, I wondered where she might be. I knew that she'd spent the afternoon with Wies and then a few hours with her mother after that. I didn't know anything about her other friends. What did she do when she stayed out until the early hours of the morning? Then I felt guilty about the fact that it was the first time Erica relayed her afternoon plans with me and it had only made me want to know more. When she gave you a finger, you wanted the whole hand. I buried my face in my pillow, and for reasons I couldn't understand, I cried.

The next evening, Erica lingered in the kitchen drying the dishes.

"When is Bas coming back?" she asked.

"He'll be back in the office on Thursday afternoon, but he has to go home to Rotterdam in the evening. Why?"

"Just because," she replied, and then, as if jumping onto another ice floe, she added, "There's a new French film at De Uitkijk. Want to go see it?"

"I'd like to, but . . ." I hesitated to tell her how tired I was. All I wanted was for the day to be over. I suddenly felt so listless, so empty, after the holiday weekend that I just wanted to go to bed early.

"What's with you?" she pressed. I could feel a conflict brewing, which was something I wanted to avoid at all costs.

"Oh, all right then. What time does it start?" I tried to sound cheerful.

"*Oh, all right then,*" she mimicked. "When Bas is here, you've got plenty of energy." I guess she'd picked up on my fatigue, but I also knew she was looking for a fight. In an effort to buy time, I closed the kitchen cupboard and wiped the counter. Then I heard myself say something I would've preferred to have kept to myself: "Listen, Erica, if Bas is the cause of this unpleasantness between us, you and I should just go our separate ways."

"Who's making it unpleasant?"

I couldn't stand the childish answer. It disgusted me to see her stoop so low. She wasn't like that.

"I might as well break up with Bas, then." It came out before I realized what I was saying, what that proposal meant.

Erica shot me a serious look. "Sorry, Bea," she said. "Sorry. It's just that . . ." she hesitated for a moment, and then said with great self-triumph, "Things were so good between us. But, of course . . . this is all nonsense. Just forget it. I had a shitty day yesterday. Ma—you know how she is. And now she's a member of the National Socialist Movement, and a passionate one at that," she laughed bitterly. "I'm still sick about it. Why don't you go to bed? I'll bring you a cup of tea."

Naturally, the superficial gesture was just her way of trimming the sails. The confidence she'd shared about Ma had been too much for her. She shooed me out of the kitchen and into my room. The battle went back underground after that. Erica was superficially friendly when we were alone and made herself scarce when Bas was around. I came to the conclusion that Bas and I weren't a good match, that he wasn't my type, that he didn't understand me, that he was actually too old and business-like for my taste. He didn't satisfy me sexually either. Even though Erica left the house when Bas stayed over (and I was increasingly tormented by the question of where she went), I had to force myself to make love to him. I just didn't need it, I told myself.

In the end, he always managed to drag me along, though without any spontaneous passion on my part. Looking back after all these years, the whole thing makes me laugh. The memory of Bas, however, has become so fuzzy that he's no longer a person to me, just a shadow in my life with Erica. But at the time, I'm sure I was telling myself that under different circumstances, our relationship could've been happy and harmonious, and maybe even for life. But I don't really blame Erica for it. Why would I?

The eruption came right before the summer. We were making vacation plans. Erica was bursting with excitement. She'd found an outlet for her restlessness—we should go somewhere together. The remainder of her inheritance was still lying untouched in the bank, and the part of my budget I hadn't put toward the equal distribution of our household budget should be—according to Erica—absolutely spent on a trip abroad. For all we knew, it could be our last chance given the international state of affairs. I would've been excited about the idea had Bas not already alluded to a prospective business trip to France, which he was hoping to extend into a vacation with me. He'd already been planning to buy a new car anyway, he said, and he would just wait until I could get some time off and we could take a road trip together. Despite the uncertainty of the times, or maybe because of it, everyone was talking about going abroad that summer. Half of the people considered the risk too great, while the other more adventurous half wanted to seize the opportunity. If there was going to be a war, and it seemed like there was going to be, people wanted to make sure they at least got to see a bit of France or Italy before it was destroyed once again by madness. One couldn't change the world order, said Bas—*après nous, le deluge.*

I hadn't accepted his invitation yet, and although I avoided the subject, I couldn't stop thinking about the trip. I liked the sound of it. Despite the shortcomings in our relationship, I had high hopes for a road trip with Bas. A chance to get away from it all, to be alone together—we'd certainly have a good time. After all, Bas was a fine person. He saw the beauty in things, he knew how to enjoy himself, he had good taste, insight . . . I envisioned the two of us driving a little English car along a country road in France (Bas would surely avoid the major highways as much as possible), rolling hills of grain on one side and old French farmhouses on the other. I imagined children playing at their front doors and mothers sitting on benches, their eldest daughters with the mending in their laps, watching us go by. We'd pass a team of oxen slowly making their way to the stable, led by a lanky boy swatting away the cruel flies with equally cruel blows to their throbbing flanks. We'd dine in the village bistro on a red gingham tablecloth, the inevitable bottle of red *vin de la maison*; or we'd sit in the shadow of a hay bale and enjoy a long, crispy baguette and cheese with a bottle of wine at our feet. These were the characteristic images of France I had in my mind, inspired by advertisements and stories I'd heard from wealthier friends. I'd never been there myself. I associated it with peace, harmony, and all the usual things one expects of a spontaneous vacation destination for happy couples. Thus, while I delighted in all my little fantasies, I saw Bas's idea—my own vacation plans—as a precursor to a difficult decision, the choice between Bas and Erica. That's not to say that I knew how it would all pan out. It was more of a dark cloud looming on the horizon, a premonition of sorts. Which is why I avoided all conversations about the upcoming holiday, both with Bas and Erica. Whenever either of them brought up the subject, I responded with a vague "yes," or by smiling and staring dreamily off into the distance. If they tried to pin me down, I'd defend myself with exaggerated protests. My office hadn't allocated vacation time yet, how could I make plans? And with my boss's health . . . I acted like the matter was completely out of my hands, as if I had no say in my vacation whatsoever, as if other people were calling the shots, and all I could do was wait for their decision. In reality, however, as the director's private secretary, and on account of my long service, I was given the first choice over other staff members. Bas added to my stress by offering to speak to my boss, to put in a good word for me. I dodged the bullet by gravely reminding him that such an intercession would reveal the nature of our relationship, something I wanted to avoid at all costs. I accused him of intruding on my private life and spoke with such indignation that he immediately retreated and apologized. Erica—and I knew it already back then—was taking advantage of the opportunity to put me in a compromised position. As summer approached, she became more and more persistent. Soon enough, not a day went by without her bringing up the topic of our vacation together, and she seemed increasingly determined. Eventually, she began talking as if we'd already decided to go somewhere together.

"Once we get to Belgium, it'll be easy to hitch a ride to France," or "I can just see us sitting in the Riviera," she'd say.

Erica had also fully convinced herself that a trip to France was actually feasible. During one of her monologues about "our trip," I let myself be so carried away that I couldn't help but mention the state of our finances.

"How are we going to pay for all this?" I asked. "We've both got five hundred guilders to our name, and it seems wiser not to spend every cent we have on this trip. We should at least keep some savings, Erica."

She was quick on the uptake. "So we're going?" she said.

"I didn't say that," I replied. "We still need to talk about it." And then, reverting back to my helpless self, I reminded her that I had to wait for my office to decide on vacation time. Erica ignored that.

"All right, let's say we've each got four hundred guilders, then. Of course, we're going to hitchhike—everybody's doing it nowadays. It's ridiculous to pay for those expensive train tickets. You get a much better view from a car anyway."

Once again, we were in dangerous waters given Bas's plan to buy a car, and she jumped right to the topic of our destination: the French Riviera. I didn't like the idea of standing on the side of the road at the mercy of passing drivers, but I decided to save my protests for later. For later? So, did that mean that deep down I'd already decided to go with Erica and not Bas? I let the actual decision be made for me. Erica and Bas had both made up their minds, in my presence but without my input, because I simply wasn't capable of deciding for myself. In all my hesitation, I let things take their course. And even when they started bickering with each other, each trying to set the other straight on where I would be spending my vacation, I stayed in the background. I was so tired of the struggle between the two of them that I refused to acknowledge the battle going on within myself. Instead, I blamed them and let the storm rage above my head.

4

As ALWAYS, it doesn't take much to set off a bomb. And once again, the holidays brought trouble. I was in a constant state of stress, this time during Pentecost. The funny thing is, in hindsight of course, I never even went to Rotterdam. I could have easily spent Sunday and Whit Monday with Bas there. The thought even occurred to me, but I didn't go. Bas lived in a boarding house, and I had already informed him at the beginning of our relationship that I didn't like the idea of sneaking around behind his landlady's back to spend the night; even if she had no problem with female visitors, as he claimed, I didn't want to be confronted by her. Bas said I was being silly but didn't press me further. I also objected to staying in a hotel. Why I was willing to share a room with Bas in France but not in Rotterdam is still a mystery to me. After all the traveling and trekking I've done these last few years, after uprooting myself from Holland completely, this objection seems incomprehensible to me now. Maybe I was more provincial and narrow-minded at the time. That might have played into it, of course, but I'm quicker to believe that I couldn't do without Erica's presence; I needed the conflict, no matter how much suffering it caused me. It's strange what we'll put ourselves through.

In the end, Bas spent Pentecost weekend in Amsterdam. He'd had a telephone installed in my room the week before as a surprise so he could call me in the evenings. Erica completely ignored the new device, and to be honest, I wasn't so thrilled about it myself. Why now? I thought, and the realization that, at least as far I was concerned, the affair was almost over while Bas still believed it to be in full bloom was deeply depressing. Every night when he called, I struggled to make conversation and ended up reformulating the same sweet nothings over and over again, which always sounded like something out of a cheap movie. Are you tired, he'd ask. Later, he remarked that by the sound of my voice you'd think I had a telephone phobia.

"I do. Didn't you know?" was my two-faced reply. Erica was sitting behind me bent over a crossword puzzle, but I could sense that she was fully immersed in our conversation.

On Whit Monday morning, just as Bas and I had sat down to a late breakfast, the phone rang. It was Erica.

"Are you doing anything special tonight?"

"No, not that I know of. Why?"

I was so rattled by the unexpected call and her sudden question that I shouted at Bas, "Are we going to do something special tonight? It's Erica!"

I could see him sitting at the kitchen table through the open bedroom door. He raised his eyebrows in surprise, hesitated, and rubbed his hand across his forehead in exhaustion. He didn't answer and I, having suddenly understood what that hand gesture meant, babbled some incoherent phrases into the phone, leading Erica to the conclusion that we had no plans. I was surprised she'd asked, I said, but open to her suggestions.

"I'll come visit and bring someone with me," she said in that self-mocking tone I'd come to know so well.

"All right," I said. I'd recovered from the shock a little bit by then and didn't want to give her the impression that I was looking forward to her visit. Still, I told her she was welcome to drop by. Back in the kitchen, Bas was clearing the table. He'd left my half-drunk cup of tea behind. I sat down and finished it, but only because I didn't know what to say. I didn't want the tea anymore.

"Strange, isn't it?" I forced myself to say.

"I'm so sick and tired of that girl." It was the first time Bas had ever given me a direct opinion about Erica, and I was thankful for it. His criticism came as a relief and broke the tension caused by all his politeness and neutrality.

"She can't help it," I said, "she doesn't know what to do with herself."

Bas gave me a long, hard look. His eyes were not reproachful, only caring and affectionate.

"And you do, missy?" He only ever called me that at night. It was a name that only felt endearing in the dark, a definition of Bas's feelings for me that always made me doubt whether I needed and wanted the security a pet name like missy afforded.

For a moment, I was tempted to drop my head down on the table and collapse into a fit of tears, thereby giving myself over to Bas and expelling the conflict from my life. I didn't though. I stood up and took my cup to the sink. I'd missed my chance, I'd have to go on alone, until the end of the long road.

That night, Erica showed up with her boss. When I saw him coming up the stairs behind her, I knew it was a child-ish attempt to compete with me. I couldn't have imagined a worse combination than Bas and Erica's boss. I never would've dreamed of bringing the two of them together, but under the circumstances, such a consideration was not to be expected from Erica. John van der Lelie was probably the only man she knew who qualified as competition. She walked in with him triumphantly. Looking back, I'm repulsed by all the little thoughts and miserable calculations that spun through my mind in that moment, but that's what it had come to. My life had been reduced to an utter mess. The whole ordeal became a lesson for later, and I've never let things reach that point again.

Bas, sweet Bas, tried to help me that night, though he had no reason to do so. I must've been a completely incompetent hostess. The next day, I had no recollection of anything that was said or how I behaved because in such painful situations people act like they're in a dream, it's almost like being drunk. The senses are half paralyzed, and you're only functioning on the outside, while the emotions swirl madly inside. I rattled on without stopping or listening to what anyone was saying, jumped from one topic to the next, and eventually just sat there in silence while the conversation went over my head. Bas was polite and let John van der Lelie have his monopoly on wisdom.

He didn't argue, he just listened with feigned interest. Erica behaved like an impresario, egging her boss on in his role as omniscient journalist. I had never seen her so devoted, and at the same time so ill at ease, especially when Van der Lelie asserted that he knew her inside out, that she was under his personal protection, and that he saw her instruction in life as his primary calling. Over coffee and cake, I felt called to point out to Van der Lelie that Erica had a lot to offer and that he was shamefully underestimating her. In response, he put a paternal hand on her knee and made reference to her youth and all the responsibilities of being a journalist. After Erica had seen him out, she barged into my room and attacked me about "that stupid comment" about her job and how I was always meddling in things that were none of my business. Bas grabbed her by the shoulders and shook her gently back and forth as if trying to calm a child having a tantrum. But Erica tore away and told him to spare her the fatherly intervention.

"Bea and I can handle this on our own. She's man enough." She shot me a challenging look, but I'd turned away and started undressing for the night. Although we weren't shy about changing in front of each other—we often saw each other half-naked—this time was different, of course, because Bas was there. Erica left the room. I'd been counting on that and had thus profited from Bas's protection. A little later we heard her march down the stairs and slam the front door behind her.

"I hope she can still catch up with Van der Lelie," Bas said dryly.

I wanted to say that Erica wasn't going to him, but I left it at that. What did I know about where she spent her nights away from home?

Later in bed, Bas took me in his arms as if nothing had happened. I pretended I was falling asleep and soon heard Bas's breath grow calm. Once again, I lay awake for hours. But this time, I crept out of bed and waited in Erica's room for sunrise. It wasn't until the next morning, during our walk along the canals, that Bas brought up the topic of the night before.

It was then that I understood that he actually was aware of our struggles. He saw through the situation better than I did— I can see that now. But since he was inhibited by an innate reticence, by tact, by the knowledge that I knew nothing, that I was groping around in the dark, he didn't help me any further.

Though I would certainly accuse him of being biased and judgmental, he stammered, he still wanted to express his opinion that Erica and I simply weren't a good fit, that living together wasn't making either of us happy. I couldn't argue with that. He was right, but I couldn't possibly explain to him that things were different before he came into our life. Our life—the realization that this was how I saw things gave me an irrevocable answer to my doubt. If I ever return to Amsterdam, the landmarks of that Whit Monday walk will still be there. The route along the Achterburgwallen is forever engraved in my memory, as if the impressions were trying to match the depth of my confusion and pain.

When we got back to the apartment, I couldn't open the door to the street. My key turned just fine in the lock, but no matter how much we fiddled and pried, the door wouldn't budge. I hopelessly rang the doorbell, but no one answered. I suspected Erica wasn't home but thought I'd try anyway. The house was completely silent. Since we were the building's only tenants (other than the offices on the ground floor, which were inevitably closed), we had no choice but to seek out a locksmith or carpenter. After a lot of effort, we finally managed to lure the plumber who lived on the street behind ours out of his house. He had the door open in no time, and despite Bas's generous tip, he still refused to repair the door for our safety. I asked Bas to go up the stairs first just in case there were any burglars inside. I was genuinely worried and waited upstairs in the hall. When Bas entered Erica's room, he let out a "Well, I'll be damned!" which was followed by Erica's sleepy greeting.

Without a word, Bas walked out of her room, past me and into the kitchen. I found him by the sink drinking a glass of water.

"Punch drunk," he said between gulps with a nod in Erica's direction. He later accused Erica of locking us out of the house on purpose, ignoring her apology that she'd been too drunk to notice what was going on and hadn't heard the doorbell ringing. The explosion—which began in the kitchen and culminated in my room—eventually got physical. I ran into my room when Bas accused Erica of being completely intoxicated. At that, she came charging into the hall, half-dazed and disheveled.

"Who you calling punch drunk, you filthy liar?"

That's how the brawl started, and it ended with Bas's departure. I curled up in the corner of my divan between the pillows. I couldn't even look up from my clasped hands, let alone intervene, when Erica attacked Bas with a chair in a fit of rage. She threw allegations, insults, and criticism in his face, and he hurled back sarcasm and insinuations. I didn't know exactly what he was saying to her. His words ricocheted off my eardrums; I didn't let them in. One month later, his voice was still echoing in my head, and shortly after that Erica confirmed that what he'd insinuated that day had been true. I didn't take sides and ended up losing Bas. I never saw him again. A few days later, I heard at the office that he'd resigned. I was the only one who knew why.

I was relieved—all the hours of regret and self-reproach couldn't change that. And to be honest, we were too busy planning our trip to France. The preparations had been endlessly drawn out and the anticipation was killing us; we were like two giddy girls planning a camping trip. Never before had we been so in tune with one another. We deliberated for hours, studied catalogs and maps and indulged our fantasies like children. But when we finally set off in late July, we left everything up to chance. Erica couldn't commit, and I knew that despite all our preparations, we were embarking on an adventure. What I didn't know was that, at least for me, the anticipation had been the best part. Even after all these years, I'll never forget the agonies of that trip.

We took the train to Paris but would later—at Erica's insistence (to which I eventually succumbed)—hitchhike down to Nice. Those few days in Paris, with that little Left Bank hotel as our home base, were over all too soon. To be honest, I was so exhausted by Erica's relentless pace that the Riviera beckoned like a sanatorium. Erica was absolutely beside herself. She only rested when she found a café terrace she liked, and even then, she fidgeted in her seat, not wanting to miss a thing, and sprang out of her chair whenever something in the distance caught her eye. Although we'd agreed once again to give each other our space, we were together all day. I soon realized that Erica was a much less conventional tourist than I was. I always need time to get used to being in a new environment and tend to seek refuge in the guidebook. I just ran around behind her and, in all honesty, felt safe by her side. She didn't seem to mind my tagging along, though she'd sometimes snarl at me when I cautiously protested her ruthless tempo or begged for an hour's rest. We visited some of the museums, but Erica's patience never lasted longer than an hour. She'd make a beeline for the paintings that interested her and then stand in front of them for fifteen minutes without a glance at the surrounding masterpieces. What she did see, she saw well and that was all that mattered to her.

"It's not like I go in Amsterdam," she argued when I protested her lack of further interest. "Loafing around museums is for snobs," she said gesturing at the crowds of tourists around us. "As if they even know why they're here! All that matters is that you've seen it."

What she was most interested in was Paris itself, the Parisians, and especially life in Montmartre and Montparnasse. She had an excellent sense of direction, and we didn't waste any time being lost. We'd wander the streets for hours, and, as if by chance, end up at places marked as points of interest in our guidebook. And she didn't appreciate advances from strangers. Whenever a man tried to make a pass at us, she'd snap his head off. Her French vocabulary may have been limited, but it was far more extensive than mine, and she had all the insults down pat. I suspected that she'd picked up these expressions during her nocturnal wanderings. Every evening, as if we'd planned it, we'd say goodbye to each other and part ways. I'd head back to our hotel, while Erica would "go out on a spree" as she liked to say. I had no idea how she survived on so little sleep. She was always the first one up in the morning and would pound on my door until I opened it. I had no idea what time she'd come home or what she'd been up to all night. I suspected that she'd been out wandering around Montparnasse and Montmartre, but, as usual, I didn't investigate any further. She was bound and determined not to waste a minute, and after each experience, or even during it, I could already feel her itching for the next one. She wanted to see everything, do everything, taste all the new drinks, try all the new foods, test every French custom, investigate every practice, experience Paris in its entirety. She was feverishly busy, both physically and mentally. Later, much later, I understood that it was during those days in Paris that she realized what she'd been missing, the thoughtless pleasure of a carefree life, a life without responsibilities, without having to be accountable to herself or anyone else. Although her upbringing and circumstances would've never allowed it, the Parisian lifestyle suited her. During those four days in Paris, she threw the ballast overboard and sounded the foghorn for the first time. She cut the anchor and cruised through Paris like a young pirate, the wind in her sails.

Our budget for the capital city was gone within two days, and we started to dip into our Riviera funds. I sent a telegram to Amsterdam to withdraw the rest of my modest savings without telling Erica. She was blind to material limitations, and I didn't want to break the spell.

5

It's no wonder I can't remember everything that happened in Paris. There was too much pressure, too much of everything. Chances are I was too exhausted for lasting impressions. I was just barely keeping up. But I do remember the afternoon we met Judy. We'd skipped breakfast, and by the time we plopped down in a little bistro, it was almost three o'clock. I was sick with hunger, but I hadn't managed to slow Erica down to appease my gnawing stomach. The restaurant was empty except for a young woman, presumably American, sitting at a corner table across from us and two couples, clearly from the countryside. By the look of them, they were on a trip they'd been saving up for for a decade. The American woman had struck up a conversation with them, and I couldn't help but notice that she was especially charming toward the two men. I could see the green light of Parisian adventure gleaming in their eyes. Their enthusiastic reciprocity was immediately dampened by their sturdy, steadfast housewives, who knew the ominous signs of twinkling eyes, red necks and agitated breathing from their own experience. They visibly froze and were soon hurrying to leave. You could tell that the woman was American by her clothes, hair, and make-up. She was *tirée,* all dolled up, as Erica said emphatically, and she was "no housecat." There was a stark contrast between her ensemble and the simple coats the two women were wearing, and Erica and I stood out next to her like two girls from the country. But if you really examine these young American women up close, the bohemians as they call them (and Paris was full of them), they're actually quite shabbily dressed and unkempt, their nonchalant chicness unarguably contrived. Erica found them interesting and attractive. Once the two couples had left, the American woman stared at us for a moment and then came over to our table.

"Do you mind if I sit down?" she asked in her bold American English. "I feel lonesome."

Erica blushed but immediately pulled up a chair. She must have told us her whole life story in less than ten minutes. She was alone in Paris and going through a divorce, but her husband had still given her a free trip to Europe that he'd gotten through a travel agency that he did legal work for. Despite the man's generosity, she didn't have one nice word to say about him.

I was floored by her candor and found her anything but likeable, but Erica was fascinated. And so, that afternoon, Judy became our third wheel. Soon enough, however, the balance shifted, and I became the third wheel. There were countless times when I was about to excuse myself, but I stayed with them. Within an hour of meeting, Erica and Judy were walking hand in hand or with their arms around each other. I couldn't believe it, but I just plodded along behind them. Their friendship was short but intense. The break-up came before dinner with such a vulgar dispute that even the Parisian passersby stopped to watch. After a "drop dead!" from Judy and an expletive from Erica, we parted ways. I didn't even know what had happened before that. There'd been some kind of little drama in the handbag department at Le Printemps, where Judy wanted to buy a gift for Erica while I discreetly perused at scarves on the other side of the store.

Out on the street, Erica took off at a brisk pace. She was visibly upset, smoking one cigarette after another as we walked in silence.

"I hope you enjoyed that," she said suddenly.

"Not particularly. What happened?"

"You wouldn't understand," she replied.

I'd felt like a beaten dog all afternoon, and that was the last straw. Without a word, I beelined for the metro station on the other side of the square and looked for the train to the hotel. I heard Erica calling after me, but ignored her. On the ride back, I sank into a depression so deep that it blinded me to all light. Maybe I knew I'd been trying to save a sinking ship. When I got back to my room, I started frantically packing my bags. In that moment, I saw myself possessed with the desire to run away from Erica, to be gone by the time she got back to the hotel. Later, I understood what I'd really wanted. I wanted Erica to be worried about me, to feel angst and remorse when she realized I'd gone. The words "loss of self-esteem" replayed over and over in my mind, leaving no room for constructive thoughts. In no time, I had dragged my suitcase and bags down the stairs. I couldn't wait for the elevator. In that latticed cage, with all its jerking and bumping, I'd fall prey to my own passivity. I needed to keep moving to save myself from the suffocating despair. I paid for my own room and when the Madame handed me the bill for Erica's, I shook my head. I knew Erica had hardly any money on her, but I didn't pay for her room. As I was walking out the door, I called over my shoulder, "*Mon amie reviendra pour ses bagages et l'addition!*" It was the only time I ever responded to Erica's behavior with a vengeful gesture. It still amazes me that I did. It wasn't until I was standing across from the hotel hailing a cab that I even thought about where I'd go. I didn't have the courage to travel on alone, so I decided to go back to Holland.

And that's when I saw Erica rushing toward the hotel. I made myself as small as possible behind a tree, but she was so set on her target that she didn't even look across the street. I just stood there. Several empty taxis drove by, but I didn't flag down any of them. I probably wasn't standing there very long, but the minutes seemed to last an eternity. It was then that I realized that there wasn't much left of the willpower I'd secretly come to rely on. Full of bitter self-contempt, I took stock of the situation. The image of Bas and Erica screaming at each other in my room over Pentecost ran through my mind, and I suddenly remembered what Bas had said to her: "My dear child, your affection for Bea is based on unhealthy emotions. You're a dangerous girl."

When Erica came back out of the hotel and looked searchingly down the street, I ran away from those words and back to her. She took my luggage and nudged me with her shoulder in the direction of a small bistro on the corner. I cried—short, painful sobs.

There were a few more dramas like that on our trip. They all seem so childish and absurd to me now. It really seemed like Judy was following us. In my better moments, my rational mind confirmed that this actually was the case. The few times

I let my disappointment get the best of me, I could always fall back on the explanation that our trip had been parallel to hers, that we were ultimately following the same route to the South. I kept telling myself that Erica—in spite of herself and through the fault of others—brought me into painful and humiliating situations. This delusion was my source of power. I'm grateful for it because it gave me a foundation on which to later build a sense of self-respect and resignation. Now, after all these years, it doesn't matter anymore. Erica's behavior has long since taken on a different meaning to me.

Erica spotted Judy in the Chartres Cathedral where she was wandering around looking bored, her eyes hidden behind outlandish red sunglasses that made her look like a clown. I still have to smile when I think of how I was more interested in the symbolism of a centuries-old wood carving of the life of Christ than in the famous stained-glass windows. As Erica and Judy sat down in a pew and settled the previous day's argument, I imagined myself as a martyr. I was so inspired by those wood-carved faces that I decided to turn the other cheek and continue south with them in Judy's Renault.

By the time we got to Tours, another fight had broken out. This time I was the cause, and even though I'm sure Erica would have preferred to take Judy's side, she remained loyal to me. In fact, she attacked Judy with such ferocity that I was completely crushed. In the space of a few weeks, I experienced three of these eruptions. Her face boiling with hate, the steam kettle whistling behind her words. I felt that she was expressing much more than what she could actually feel in that moment, more than what the situation called for. During those spats with Judy, I always had to suppress, in addition to my astonishment, a sensation of hilarity. The level of emotion they displayed was ridiculous. Later in life, I realized that women in Erica's presence, both those she loved and those she despised, had a tendency to sway toward extremes. Erica and Judy acted like two little girls—one minute they were hitting and scratching each other and the next they were wrapped in each other's arms and sharing their deepest secrets, promising to be friends forever. I wasn't used to it yet back then.

In Tours, I managed to regain some control by refusing Judy's offer to treat us to lunch at the most expensive restaurant. Our budget was calculated for bread, wine, and cheese picked up along the route or, if necessary, at a village inn, and only I knew where the money for those simple meals was coming from. Although I wasn't prepared to reveal the secret of our fatter wallet, I didn't want to spend my precious savings on unnecessary excesses just to keep up with Judy. And I wasn't about to accept the perks of her financial position either. Later, when we hitched a ride with an English couple, Erica called me a bluestocking and an old stick in the mud, which was surely meant as a joke. We enjoyed the ride. The couple, though British and thus reserved by nature, proved friendly and attentive and let us tag along with them to Nice. We had to be at their hotel at a certain time in the morning to go, but otherwise they left us alone and provided us with nothing more than the back seat of their car. We were really lucky, and those three days were ideal.

In Nice, things took another turn for the worse. Erica developed a passion for roulette—a fascination I feared. Still, I went along and enjoyed watching and philosophizing. But then Judy showed up again. After she and Erica had thrown their arms around each other's necks, they were once again attached at the hip. I have to admit that Judy's Renault was a major plus. We drove along the entire coast all the way to the Italian border, and I managed to stay out of their way by isolating myself. I was the neutral spectator, a position I forced myself into and maintained with vigilance despite many moments of misery. This was the only way to keep the expedition possible and my position unassailable. On the outside, I was completely detached from Erica, and I doubt she noticed my inner struggle. Every once in a while, she'd toss a little friendship in my direction and I accepted it without making a scene. She sought these brief moments of contact with me whenever she needed a witness to confirm the reality of her glorious experiences.

Within a day or two of arriving in a new place, I'd branch off on my own. We'd set a departure time, and then I'd head out to explore. Of course, Erica and Judy rarely bothered to look at a clock, and I spent hours waiting for them. But at least I was able to discover the things that interested me without the torture of their company. It was mainly the evenings that were a problem. Erica just couldn't get enough of the roulette table. Sometimes we had to drive miles to the nearest casino, where Erica and Judy would be swallowed up at the entrance, and I would end up wandering around outside. Later I'd overhear in their conversation whether they'd won or lost. That's how I figured out that Judy was giving Erica cash to play with.

Those cool, fragrant nights alone in my hotel room seemed to last an eternity. I couldn't sleep. Even the soothing powders I'd bought from a pharmacist in Nice didn't calm me down. Since we only had sixteen days of vacation, and Erica still insisted on seeing everything, we kept tearing around. When I think back on my memories from the Côte d'Azur, I still see that gray Renault tearing down the boulevards, Judy behind the wheel, Erica next to her, me in the backseat. The "resort town" that had seemed so alluring in Paris turned out to be (in reality and in my memory) nothing but a merry-go-round. I know I spent hours lying on the beach, but I can't picture it anymore. Sometimes I saw Erica and Judy lying there with their arms around each other frying in the sun or tossing a big rubber ball back and forth in their short French bathing suits, shouting like happy schoolgirls, their suntanned bodies glistening with oil. If they spotted me, they'd call out a nonchalant "Hello," but most of the time I managed to pass unseen.

I started avoiding the fashionable boulevards after they deliberately ignored me once on a café terrace. Blinded by the bright sunlight, I didn't recognize them at first. There, sitting under an awning, was a group of women, American and French by the look of them, drinking Pernod with a studied look of boredom on their faces. The group consisted of a strapping, middle-aged butch woman in a sailor's sweater and six young girls dressed and coifed with a refinement intended to set them apart from less complicated souls. I scanned the circle and spotted Erica and Judy. They exchanged a quick look of warning and then Erica greeted me with a faint smile. I turned around and rushed off. It was a pitiable retreat, and the humiliation of it stuck with me for a long time. After that, the boulevards were nothing more than routes to the beach to me, and I decided to limit my wanderings to the villages and seaside resort areas. Looking back, I see those long walks in Antibes, Cagnes, St. Paul, Villefranche like a cinemagoer who hardly notices the extras climbing the stairs to the cathedral, standing at the gate of the town hall, walking toward the camera on a country road. And what the extra thinks or feels, despite the bounce in her step and the cheerful look on her face, is of no importance.

The day we were supposed to head home, Erica bluntly informed me that she was going to stay on a bit. Judy, who was there when she made the announcement, shot me a challenging look, but I didn't respond.

"*Call the paper and tell them I'm extremely sick*," Erica said in her best American English. "*Tell them something, I don't care what.*" It was true—she didn't care, and the decision not to return home on time didn't cause her the least bit of stress. Even though the end of the vacation had been hanging over her head the entire time, and she'd filled our days as a result, when the moment of departure arrived, she simply couldn't bring herself to go. As a concession to me, she persuaded Judy to drive me to the station in Nice. It was a sign that she at least felt a little bit guilty on my account, but I was too defeated to think about it. After a cold goodbye in front of the station, they drove off, and I followed the porter with my luggage.

6

ERICA WAS GONE until the end of August. She later confessed to me that she'd been forced to return to Amsterdam after Judy had rushed home to America due to the threat of war. I didn't hear anything from her the entire time she was away. I checked the mailbox three times a day for a letter or even a postcard. In the morning, I'd listen for the arrival of the morning post, and when my inner turmoil got the best of me around lunchtime, I'd even go home to check the midday delivery as well. Then, in the evening, I'd find myself watching out the window for the mailman. As the international crisis escalated and fears of a German invasion grew, so did my concern for Erica. The crisis actually served as an excuse for my distress and made it possible for me to talk about Erica's absence with my friends and colleagues at work. To be honest though, the world around me could've gone up in flames, and I still would've been more worried about the conflict between Erica and me. I was consumed by my own troubles. It's always that way, isn't it? War offers a way out for people who've been backed into a corner, who no longer see any salvation or future for themselves, and who quietly hope for an external tragedy to come along and put an end to the unbearable situation they've found themselves in.

That year, the world was pushed to the brink of collapse, but I hardly thought about the atrocious events happening in Spain, Austria, Munich, and Asia. I was running in circles around my own experiences and problems, like a horse in a ring, blinders preventing me from seeing anything other than Erica in front of me, while I was unable, unworthy, of catching up to her. Finally, I had an outlet for my tormented thoughts. I used the international crisis as a cover to tell everyone I knew about my concern for Erica. I even went so far in my self-delusion as to call the paper where she worked. Van der Lelie advised me to contact the consul in Nice. He even offered to send a telegram himself. Perhaps they'd know whether Erica had been admitted to a hospital.

"I actually wanted to call you," he said pompously. "I'm terribly worried about her myself." I guess he'd bought my story about Erica being sick.

When the call came for general mobilization on August 29, I was on the brink of a nervous breakdown, but by one o'clock the next afternoon, Erica was standing in front of me. She'd come home by plane, and her enthusiastic report of her first flight neutralized the conflict between us. Pretty soon, she was running down the stairs to go to work. All of a sudden, she was in a hurry to get to the office on time. A few minutes later, when I was walking along the canal to the tram stop, I saw her riding her bike around the corner, as if she'd never been away.

That evening, I made dinner, as always, while she sat there and said, "I acted like an animal, Bea, but there was nothing I could do about it. It was all too heavenly. Forget it, if you can, and if you can't, then let me have it right now, come on, give it to me, but whatever you do, don't keep looking at me with those sad puppy eyes."

That was that, as far as she was concerned. I devoured my food, told her I had an appointment, and left the house as soon as the dishes were done. I wandered through the old town until midnight, and when I finally came home, I'd seemingly won the battle with myself. I can now admit that I was so happy to have Erica back that the whole inner struggle had been an act, a comedy I'd performed for myself, an attempt to write a suitable ending to the drama.

Our lives went back to normal—except that thick envelopes from America arrived several times a week, and Erica was spending a lot of time writing letters.

That fall, she had no trouble staying busy. Maybe she lived off the vestiges of her satisfying summer. Maybe all the excitement and restlessness provided a distraction from the tense political situation. There was so much was going on at home and abroad that Van der Lelie was forced to make use of Erica's skills. She often worked overtime, and by October she was working the night shift. She came home increasingly wound up with all kinds of crazy stories and for the first time since I'd known her, she had an outspoken opinion about fascism and the Nazis. True to form, she jumped to extremes and rattled our apartment with her fiery speeches. There was no limit to her hate for the Germans, and Ma, as the closest opponent within her reach, bore the brunt of it.

"Get a load of this, Bea—that stupid bitch—it's unbelievable, she says that Hitler is going to save Europe. You should hear her rant about the Jews. It's because Pa's one of them. Did I ever tell you that? It's true—I'm half-Jewish. But, anyway, maybe that's not even it, though she'd be more than happy to see him drop dead. She's stupid, Bea, and disappointed with her life, exactly the kind of person that gets sucked into all that stuff. My mother, of all people!"

And then she closed with: "She's not welcome in this house anymore, remember that."

I hadn't seen Ma in months, and with all her political activities I assumed she didn't have time to visit her daughter anyway. But it didn't occur to Erica that if her mother just showed on our doorstep one day unannounced, I wouldn't be able to refuse her. And oddly enough, Erica was still visiting her. Most likely she couldn't resist the temptation to use her political combativeness as a means of telling her mother the truth, to vent her long-suppressed contempt. There were no more jokes about her mother. She even started sharing stories from her past with me, and they were anything but cheerful. It was through Erica's reaction toward her mother, the National Socialist, that I came to understand how much contempt, hatred, and pent-up aggression were behind those jokes Erica used to make. She seemed to find those tempestuous visits with her mother deeply satisfying.

That November she was recruited by a charitable organization that went down to meet Jewish children fleeing Germany at the Dutch border. She also attended political meetings, including those of the Dutch Nazi party, where she liked to stir up trouble and—as she told me with childlike pride—got herself thrown out from time to time.

"I hope Ma saw that," she said.

"Was she there?" I asked.

"Probably. That bitch has gone completely crazy."

"What does the General have to say about it?"

"That's another thing! He's just like her, of course. You've met him, haven't you?"

To Erica, you were either good or you were in the NSB—
the National Socialist Movement—and she had an opinion
about everyone.

"He could be one," she'd say about any given person.
"Either he's already a Nazi or he'll be one soon." Most of her
suspects were innocent citizens, but there were a few cases
where her assessment was spot on.

I was averse to all the commotion and tried to keep my
distance. Nevertheless, Erica sometimes talked me into doing a
bit of administrative work, which she took on but never carried
out, or got me to read the books and pamphlets she brought
home with her. I've never had much respect for political fanati-
cism. Even then, I had little faith in humanity, and now that I'm
in my forties, I know for a fact that when people get on their
soapboxes (as they say here in America), they're driven more
by haste than goodwill. Erica was trying to populate the lonely
steppes of her life with friends and enemies, but whenever I
tried to express this, she'd rip me to shreds. Once she accused
me of always seeing the worst in people and said that I had no
love in me. These ruthless words upset me for days. I knew I'd
changed, that I'd grown bitter, and silently I blamed Erica for it.

But soon enough, Erica gave up her political ambitions.
Her charity was no match for Van der Lelie's intrigues, and she
threw down her weapons as quickly as she'd taken them up.
Suddenly, she was back at home, and she didn't say another
word about the dangers of Nazism. Only after about a week
did she relay what had happened in bits and pieces. I wasn't
at all surprised to learn that Van der Lelie was in the NSB. If
you asked me, that black shirt suited him. There were already
plenty of rumors flying around about the newspaper's political

sympathies, and Van der Lelie had nothing to lose by forcing Erica to choose between her political convictions and her job. At that point, I took a combative stance and told her I was surprised that she'd backed down so easily. At first, she made all kinds of excuses. Van der Lelie had threatened her, said he'd make it impossible for her to get a job anywhere else, that he wouldn't write her any letters of recommendation, that he'd give her a bad reference and warn people about her. He'd told her that if she ever got a job at another newspaper, she'd have to work her way up from the bottom again; that she wouldn't earn enough, that there were no other jobs in journalism for women, that the political world could do without her, and finally, "What does it matter anyway?" Of course, I didn't accept any of these excuses, but I let it drop. Erica looked so miserable and seemed so depressed that I left her alone. She spent the entire Sunday in bed, something she hadn't done for a long time. Her inexplicable behavior kept me up at night. I couldn't make any sense of it. Was she still in love with Van der Lelie? Had she surrendered just to keep his interest? Or had the disillusionment of finding out that he was in the NSB been too much for her? What a child she still was!

Wies started calling repeatedly. She'd never called the house before, at least not to my knowledge. She asked where Erica was, what time she'd be home, if I ever saw her. I answered to the best of my knowledge and passed her messages along to Erica, who wasn't interested. Even if she was home, she shooed away the phone and told me to tell Wies that she wasn't there. The first time Wies called, I assumed she and Erica still saw each other, and from the next few calls, I concluded that she had turned to Wies for comfort and support in her crisis. So why was she avoiding her calls? I was completely lost. How innocent I was! But how could I have known that Van der Lelie had taken advantage of what he thought he knew about Wies and Erica's relationship in order to put Erica on the chopping block? It never occurred to me that she was being blackmailed. I hardly knew what blackmail was. It was just a word I'd picked up somewhere but that had no place in my vocabulary. From where I stood, I just couldn't see that Erica, who was so much younger than me, who always seemed so childish with all her whims and immaturities, her boyish haircut, sloppy boy's shirts and silly knee socks, had exposed herself to someone with a knife up his sleeve.

After a week or so, Erica gave me the task of telling Wies that she was very busy but that she would write to her. Submissively, I carried out the task. The words provoked a brief silence on the other end of the line followed by a derisive laugh. That was the end of it. Wies's name didn't come up again until months later, when Erica didn't have any secrets from me anymore.

"Take that whole situation with Wies, for example," she said.

"It was sexually innocent, though we often slept together in the same bed. I didn't do it back then, you know. But Van der Lelie scared the shit out of me, so I didn't dare meet up with Wies again. He saw right through me before I'd even figured it out myself. His accusation was kind of a revelation to me. Jesus, I'll never forget those weeks."

"What about Judy?" I asked.

"I was naïve, Bea. For Judy, those kinds of things are more of an adventure. She can take it or leave it. She made it an adventure for me too. You wouldn't understand."

Erica would never forget those weeks, but neither would I. You would've thought she was sick. Her skin turned a pale shade of yellow and dark circles formed under her eyes. The lines around her mouth became even more pronounced and thin grooves appeared in her skin. She barely ate and, as far as I could tell, didn't sleep at all.

Whenever I woke up in a panic, I'd see her light still on behind the sliding doors. I couldn't help her. Our conversation was limited to my encouragements to eat and general remarks about the house and weather, which she responded to with a snarl and a single word respectively. Gradually, her restlessness gave way to depression. But this time Erica wasn't looking for distraction. She did her work at the newspaper and spent the rest of her time at home. The letters from America stopped coming, and Erica stopped writing. She just lay on her bed and stared out the window for hours. It was almost as if she were afraid to leave the house. She didn't even want to go to the movies anymore, so I went alone. It bothered me, but I still went out every now and then. The atmosphere in the house was unbearable, and sometimes I just couldn't take it anymore. Whenever I was out, however, I felt restless and yearned for the apartment. Of course, Erica eventually came around, which awakened in her a longing for change and the constant need to be busy.

7

NOT LONG AFTER THAT, on a warm Sunday in October, we went for a walk in the dunes. The weather had turned cold already, and I took shelter behind a fisherman's house while Erica stood out on the beach staring at the sea. A late blackbird, lost out there on the coast, captured my attention for a while. It occurred to me that Erica was like that bird, unable to decide where to land, under the roof of the house—where faces appear behind windows, where a voice, a laugh, a strange sound all pose a potential threat—in this tree or that tree, on the gutter of a shed or in the safety of the woods. She was constantly flying back and forth, anxiously flapping her wings, and then with a graceful swoop, she'd start all over again.

"You know," Erica said when she returned, "we're living all wrong. We should've rented a house by the sea. Let's give up our apartment and commute."

"Yes," I said, "good idea." It was easy enough to say in that moment because soon she'd forget all about it. There was no need to get into details. She always had some new proposal that would never be executed. All her plans, all her restlessness, always waiting for . . . for what?

But this time I'd miscalculated. I didn't think anything of Erica's behavior the following week. Of course, I'd noticed she was in a more cheerful mood, and I was happy to have a bit of peace and harmony in the house for a few days, happy to see her happy. On Saturday, she announced that she'd be gone all day on Sunday and that I shouldn't wait up for her. As usual, I didn't ask questions and when I woke up at ten o'clock the next day, she'd already left.

I spent the day alone, treated myself to breakfast in bed, wrote some letters, read, and enjoyed my solitude. In the afternoon, I decided to go to the Rijksmuseum, but when I found myself surrounded by couples and families shuffling past the paintings and suits of armor, I was overcome by a strange sense of loneliness. I thought of Erica, missed her even, though this feeling bothered me, and I tried to suppress it. I had forced myself to visit the museum—after all, you have to do something, you can't just spend the whole day at home. There, under the high vaulted ceilings, among people enjoying the company of their family or beloved (at the time it all seemed so ideal to me), I wondered why I hadn't just stayed in my room where I felt safe. Why had I forced myself to come here? Was the need to be constantly active starting to get to me as well? Or was I afraid that Erica would judge me for spending an entire Sunday at home by myself? Maybe I was afraid of her disdain, her contempt, which I'd been exposed to a lot in those days. I felt suffocated by that same feeling of abandonment that had grabbed me by the throat in France and deprived me of all sensation during my solitary walks through the coastal villages. I gazed at the paintings by Rembrandt and Vermeer with feigned interest, so acutely aware of the people around me that I was oblivious to the scenes on the canvas. I envied and feared those people because they accentuated my tense state of mind. I was a pitiful sight and the image of myself that Erica would throw in my face hours later was probably already running through my mind.

At around seven o'clock, just as I was spooning some leftovers onto my plate, Erica came stomping up the stairs. So, she's still in a good mood, I thought, and probably full of cheerful stories.

"Done! All worked out," she said and sank into a chair at the kitchen table.

"Have you eaten?" I asked with a hand on the bread box.

"Too excited," she said, "I'll eat later, don't worry about it. I GOT US A PLACE BY THE SEA! In Egmond! Got really lucky!"

"You got us a what? Where?" I was so caught off guard that all I could do was take out the bread and rummage around in the drawer for a bread knife.

"We're going to live in Egmond aan Zee," she said. "I'll need the money right away; I've got to send the deposit tomorrow. They already gave me the key. Really nice people, they just trusted me." She pulled a shiny new key out of her jacket and dangled it in front of me. "It's still under construction, we can move in next month." This was a completely senseless maneuver following a period of defeat. An act of desperation, I thought to myself. A wild leap at the end of a period of inertia she was no longer able to endure.

I sat down at the kitchen table.

"My god, Erica—how could you . . ."

But that was as far as I got. She seemed so happy. The bird had finally chosen a place to perch. I didn't want to discourage her, not then, maybe in a few hours I would ask some cautious questions and then try to bring her back to reality later that evening. Egmond, how far was that from Amsterdam by train? Maybe there was a bus, I thought irritably. And how in the world were we going to get out of our lease?

"What is it now?" she said. "Are you going to put a damper on things again? You're such an old nag, Bea. You haven't got the nerve, no guts at all. This—" she said with a sweeping gesture around our kitchen, at the knife I was thoughtlessly holding in my hand. "This isn't life! You've got to make something of it. Dare to live!" She seemed to like that theme and latched onto it. "We live here like two parakeets on a perch. Same thing every day. We're not that young anymore, you know. How many years have we wasted? Especially you. You're older than I am. What've you got to show for it? An office job. And there you are with your bread knife in your little kitchen with your little checkered curtains and checkered tablecloth. So lovely, that red! How original! And Wednesday night you're invited out for pancakes with Dottie and Max and their snot-nose kids. Flapjacks *and* whining children! What a treat! Saturday night we'll go to the movies, and then on Sunday maybe we'll walk over to Café Klein Kalfje. Look at you, with your new Sunday dress, with that little scarf. Isn't life beautiful, full of surprises and cups of tea. After all this time with you, I'm becoming that way too. I hadn't even noticed myself. We're two old spinsters living upstairs." She cursed and slammed the table with her fist. "I've got to get out. Maybe I need to get away from you. This is no life for me." Then, she remembered her new plan: "We'll move to Egmond. That I'll try. At least it's something."

I cut myself on the jagged edge of the bread knife; I'd been sliding it up and down my finger throughout the entire eruption. I licked away the blood and sucked the wound. What now? What should I say?

"Well, Erica," I began soothingly, but she wrenched the knife from my hands and began banging around in the kitchen to make herself dinner. Two hunks of bread, a lump of cheese, a glass of beer.

"Let me just . . ." I stood halfway out of my chair. At that, she threw everything down, glared at me with her hate-filled eyes and stormed out. I just sat there for a moment, my heart pounding. The slam of the kitchen door echoing in my ears.

Later, when I was still pacing nervously around my room, I heard her in the kitchen again. I guess she got hungry—I had to let her have her way. I couldn't help but think about the dainty little sandwiches I'd been planning to make with yesterday's steak, with pickles and thin slices of tomato, all elegantly arranged on a colorful plate, and—as a surprise—mini pastries bought on my way home from the museum. That was the lunch I'd imagined for us, but I hadn't been allowed to serve it. I shouldn't have spoiled her so much. I shouldn't have forced my care on her like that. No wonder she'd gotten angry. I had to let her be free, in that way too. Then I saw myself wandering around the museum and a vestige of the pain I'd felt echoed through my stomach. Instinctively, I touched my new scarf, and the stifled sobs brought some relief. Erica had cut me deeply. I'd bought the silk scarf from Liberty. It had been too expensive, but I thought it would brighten up last winter's dark blue dress. I saw myself walking around that museum so clearly—after all, you've got to *do* something—but in reality, all I'd done was expose myself to unnecessary torture, loneliness, the abnormal reaction of a stressed-out person. What had happened to me? I didn't understand it at the time.

In the end, we moved to Egmond aan Zee. I can't re-member everything that happened in the three weeks before the moving truck pulled into our new hometown. I remember sitting there on a folded horse blanket, surrounded by all our belongings, a musty tarp from the moving company over my head and shoulders against the steady drizzle, utterly powerless against the heavy depression that descended on the rumbling truck just as it started to rain. Erica was sitting in the front seat between the movers with a girl named Dolly in her lap. I'd never met this Dolly person before and didn't even know she existed. They seemed to be having a good time. Occasionally, they'd laugh in my direction. I felt like a piece of furniture, dragged into Erica's flight from herself. I was so exhausted from all the tension and silent hostility between us before I'd finally given in, from all the trouble with the Amsterdam apartment, from all the packing, that the complications of living outside the city seemed insurmountable to me. Halfway through the trip, Erica stopped the truck and offered to switch seats. I refused and said I was enjoying the open landscape.

"It's like a movie, Erica, everything"—I waved my arm—"just rolls away, it's wonderful."

No, I didn't want to interrupt the adventure, I said. I was so well cast in my role in our little comedy that Erica, convinced by my response, climbed happily back into the front seat. Now I really have to enjoy it, I thought.

The classic Dutch polder landscape, uninterrupted by trains and cars, was indeed impressive, and the gray weather made it all the more dramatic. But my attempt to focus on the scenery failed miserably. I was so irritated by Dolly's unexpected presence that my last bit of courage was splashed away like a soap bubble. I was in too low of spirts. Why had Erica invited her? She certainly wasn't the type of person you'd ask to help with a move or someone who, aware of her own efficiency, would be eager to lend a hand. Still, she'd reported for duty that morning at seven o'clock. She'd barely lifted a finger, but she did drive me to despair with all her pseudo-cosmopolitan remarks and anecdotes about people I didn't know. When we arrived in Egmond, in the midst of all the chaos, she made herself comfortable in an easy chair. It was up to me to go get us some coffee, even that was too much for her. While I was running around in the rain looking for a café or an inn, I wondered whether Dolly would be the next Judy. The future seemed so bleak that I was already imagining Dolly as a regular guest at our house, and me sitting alone in Egmond while Erica was out having fun with her in Amsterdam. What did Erica see in her? I sized her up against myself, and as far as I could tell (with all my Dutch snobbery), I was by far superior: I came from a better background, had more to offer, was more intelligent. On the other hand, maybe I was out of the running because I was too stiff or boring or bland. What did Erica want in a friend? Why did she want to live with me when she so clearly preferred these gaudy, superficial, outspoken girls like Judy and Dolly? The two women were certainly of the same caliber.

I hurried back with an old thermos full of coffee from the friendly grocer's wife. It felt warm in my freezing hands. Maybe the kindness of the simple villagers would do us good. With that hopeful thought, the world seemed a bit rosier. And then it occurred to me—a thought which was problematic in itself but optimistic given my current situation—that Erica had invited Dolly to serve as a lightning rod. Maybe she'd thought the day would be easier with a neutral person there. Was Erica afraid to be alone with me? Despite the stubbornness with which she'd pushed the moving plan forward, she might have known that I was right, that moving to Egmond was insane and that she shouldn't have dragged me into it.

Over the next few weeks, she didn't show any signs of regret; however, in the long run, my gloomy predictions turned out to be correct. Erica couldn't stand it there. Just as I'd gotten settled into the modern bedroom Erica had assigned to me, with its giant windows to the sea, just as I'd resigned myself to getting up early and traveling back and forth to Amsterdam, just as I'd made my peace with evenings as monotonous as the steadily crashing waves and ventured to draw Erica into my happiness, her restlessness reared its head once again, bringing with it a new sense of dissatisfaction. We started going out in the evenings, chatting with the fishermen on the corner, drinking in the local bar (while the locals eyed us with suspicion), getting to know the women in the shops, and even visited a young painter Erica had met on the train. Pretty soon, our evenings in the village turned into bus trips to the movie theater in Alkmaar. Finally, there came a week when we were only at the apartment to sleep—an absurd series of train and bus trips between Amsterdam and Egmond all for five hours of sleep in our dusty, neglected apartment. I was too tired to work, too stressed and unhappy to sleep. At breakfast on Monday, I announced that I intended to come straight home to Egmond after work that week and stay there. Erica took note and went out alone. Apparently, she had more fun without me, and once I'd managed to get over the thought of her in Amsterdam with Dolly, who had seemingly disappeared from our lives after moving day, or in the dimly lit village or in the Alkmaar cinema, I actually enjoyed the quiet weeks in my cozy room with my books, knitting, and household chores. Sometimes after I got home in the evening, I'd go for a walk along the sea at dusk with a sandwich or a few pieces of fruit in my coat pocket in case I got hungry. I'd eat dinner when I got home after dark. I was fairly happy. I especially liked the weekends, which I mostly spent alone. My appearance improved, and I felt rested and full of life. I took on the role of house mother, did the shopping as soon as I got off the bus, kept the apartment clean, washed and ironed our clothes. Yes, Erica's too, as I'd often do in later years. Erica was still nonchalant about her appearance, and despite my best efforts, she looked like a sloppy teenage boy. We barely saw each other; I didn't even wait for her in the morning. Before the bus left, I'd wonder half-amused whether she'd actually make it. Occasionally she did miss the bus, which meant she'd also miss the train connection in Castricum.

In the back of my mind, I felt a vague sense of pity, but it wasn't strong enough to worry about, or rather I didn't let it get to me. I simply didn't want to think about it.

One night while reading in bed, I actually heard her come in, which meant she was home earlier than usual. Usually I was asleep and didn't hear the sound of her footsteps outside my door. This time she stumbled around the house, waiting for me to come out and greet her. When that didn't work, she knocked on my door and asked if I was asleep yet. I said no (an answer I would later come to regret), and she came in. In the light of my reading lamp, I saw that she was as pale as a sheet and the dark circles had reappeared under her eyes. Even her tough constitution had been unable to cope with the restlessness of recent weeks.

"It's hot in here," she said and pulled off her sweater.

"Central heating," I replied with the grimace we'd used in the beginning to show our respect for the new building's modern installations. She was wearing a dirty blouse even though I'd been up late ironing the night before and had placed a pile of clean shirts—the same boyish ones she always wore—in her closet. She looked disheveled, as if she hadn't changed clothes in days. She sat at the foot of my bed and looked straight at me, one eye squinting through the smoke of her cigarette.

"I come with the peace pipe," she said, and trying to be funny, she took the cigarette between her thumb and index finger and held it at eye level between us.

Several possible responses flashed through my mind, but they all seemed inadequate or too open to interpretation. So I just smiled, though I would've liked to have said something. We sat there for a moment, me leaning against the pillows, and Erica, still eyeing me closely. It was always this way. Whatever happened, Erica showed no fear, none of the embarrassment that comes from shame and guilt. Once she was ready to show her cards, clear the air, admit her mistakes, she did so with no qualms whatsoever. Now I know that in those moments she'd already settled the matter within herself. The confrontation with me was more of an afterthought. Deep down, Erica was accountable to no one but herself.

"I have to work the night shift again next month. I talked to Betsie," she said and then cut to it. "She wants two weeks to find another apartment and then we can move back in. We'll cover the moving costs."

"You're out of your mind, you're crazy." Those were the only words I could find. It was unbelievable. How could she accept no responsibility whatsoever? Where did she find the nerve to ask Betsie, an office acquaintance of mine who had taken over our lease in Amsterdam, to give us back the apartment after only two months? And Betsie was no pushover either. A fairly aggressive woman in her forties, she'd been very firm and business-like about our first transaction and even insisted on drawing up a sublease agreement. And now, as if it were the most normal thing in the world, Erica had persuaded her to clear out because Erica wanted to go back. Another victim had succumbed to her whims. And I was simply at her disposal. The anger boiling up inside me was so intense that I couldn't take it lying down. I threw off the blankets and reached for my kimono on the chair next to the bed. But Erica was quicker than me. She pulled the covers back up and pushed me back with her hands on my chest. I looked at her smiling above me, inhaled that familiar aroma of lavender soap and cigarette smoke I'd always liked so much. But suddenly I couldn't stand it. The pressure of her strong hands brought me outside myself. I kicked her off me with my drawn-up knees and began shouting uncontrollably—curses, swears, every abuse I could think of. She let go of me immediately and returned to the foot of the bed. The outburst calmed me, and I sank back into the pillows ashamed of my rage.

"You really know how to push someone to the edge," I said, as if I'd prepared the phrase beforehand. "You do whatever you want with no thought whatsoever about me."

At first, Erica didn't say anything. She studied her fingernails, and I couldn't see her face. Then, all of a sudden, she threw herself onto the bed with her face in the blankets. She didn't cry, she just lay there motionless for what seemed like an eternity. I didn't know what to do. Then I felt her hands on my hips and her head against my loins.

"Bea," she said, her voice smothered against me. "Bea, don't you get it?"

The tears came moments later in an explosion of anger, hate, and disappointment. She accused me of misleading her, of driving her to confess, of letting her have her way and then humiliating her with my rejection. There was nothing for me to say. How innocent, no, how blind and stupid I'd been. I thought of Bas, of his accusations toward Erica on his last visit. In an effort to save myself from the chaos of my own thoughts, no, from my very existence in that moment, I concentrated all my emotions on Erica. Poor, twisted Erica. But I couldn't bring myself to touch her, to comfort her. Never again, I thought with revulsion. Or was it fear? Despite what had happened, I didn't really feel repulsed by her, because even then, in that moment, I knew I hadn't stopped her advances, that I'd let her—as she put it—have her way. It came as a terrifying surprise, because even then I felt for her, I felt her humiliation and would've liked to have comforted her, to have laid my hands on her shiny boyish head as she stood there sobbing against the leg of a chair in helpless misery.

"This is the way I am!" she screamed. "This is the way I am!" She turned toward me, her face wet with tears and contorted into an expression of equal parts pain and triumph. "And it's the way you are too. Yes, you, Bea. Admit it! Just admit it!" Gasping between sobs, but with a sense of triumph in her voice, the triumph of a world conqueror, she repeated the injunction over and over again. I sprang out of bed, my whole body shaking, and ran (looking back it all seems so ridiculous) into the kitchen, the only hiding place within reach.

Hours later we found each other back in my room, calmer, avoiding each other's gaze. Erica talked until the sun came up. It wasn't a plea, why would she defend herself? The fact that she was suffering from what I, with all my superiority and compassion (really just forms of self-preservation), referred to as an abnormality was even more evident that night than during the weeks when she'd been so tormented by the discovery of her wrongness. Wrong, that's what she called it that night. It was catharsis that compelled her to try to reconcile herself with her wrongness. After that night, she never referred to herself that way again. She resigned herself to a nature that couldn't be changed, accepted the consequences and enjoyed her life. I've always admired that. But that night I stood at the window with my back to her—how could I ever confront her openly again? I stared blindly at the moonlit sea and saw nothing but scenes from Erica's unhappy childhood. Her experiences over the past year, of which I'd suspected little or nothing until that night, were suddenly so clear that it was as if I'd experienced them myself. My immediate powers of observation failed me until I suddenly became aware of the morning mist on the water and the gray, deserted beach. Now I knew everything. But for what? Erica's confession and the accusation against me had driven us irrevocably apart, I thought. We were now forced to go our separate ways, living together had become impossible. But less than a month later I came to the equally irrevocable conviction that we were bound together for life, that our short year together had been, at least for me, decisive. I could no longer live without her, and with her there was nothing but the strange existence that had been predetermined for her by her miserable youth, in which I could only participate in as a witness.

8

THE NEXT MONTH I was alone in Egmond, more alone than I'd ever been in my life. After that night, Erica packed a suitcase and left, where to I didn't know. As soon as the door closed behind her, I took a bath. I scrubbed away the caresses of her authoritative hands, her compelling mouth, the scent of lavender and cigarette smoke that lingered on my skin. I changed my bedsheets and left for Amsterdam. But when I got off at Central Station, I realized that the entire world had changed, I couldn't go back to the office. As someone who'd always had a strong sense of duty, I tried to convince myself that I had to go to work, that the normalcy of my job would do me good, better than doing nothing, but I couldn't. Still, I forced myself to go, even got on the tram, but then I got off halfway.

The stop was near the Rijksmuseum, so I went in. Why do we do these things to ourselves? Was I trying to make myself even more bitter? Was I searching for the deepest misery I could find? This time the museum was quiet. The only people there that early in the morning were the copyists and a few ambitious tourists. After a while, I wandered into a gallery where a group of girls from the countryside were sitting with a woman who was presumably their drawing teacher, soaking up the dose of culture that schools feel called on to provide. I watched them for a moment, clinging to the distraction they offered me. Most likely, the giggling and whispering had already started that morning, when they woke up at the boardinghouse for Christian women. After several fits of stifled laughter over breakfast in the cafeteria, about a goofy waiter or snippety waitress, they were temporarily brought to order by a calming, pedagogical speech from their teacher. Now that they were in the museum, they'd lost control again—everything seemed strange and ridiculous, and there was no other outlet for their excitement. Even Rembrandt's masterpieces, which seemed so foreign compared to the reproductions on their birthday calendars at home, gave rise to uncontrollable giggling. It re- minded me of my own field trips to Amsterdam when I was in school. And Erica? Now I knew what kind of youth she'd had. Of course she hadn't joined in on the giggling, because her breathless excitement was fixated elsewhere—on the young female director who had unexpectedly chaperoned the school trip. Furious about the other girls' childish horseplay, Erica would have stayed at the director's side, consumed by the rigid attentiveness and complete absorption that comes only from love. For Erica, ever the serious tomboy, school had always been a refuge, and in the last year it became her haven. There, she finally found the love she'd been missing. There, at least for most of the day, she was safe from her mother's selfishness, grudges and hysteria, from the woman she'd be powerlessly handed over to after her father walked out.

Things aren't fairly distributed in this world. The relationship between Erica and her parents was a bitter farce, a sinister joke of fate—especially in the years before her father left, when the only way he could stand his wife was by escaping to the corner bar. That was back before their child could find shelter at school. Erica was either trapped in a house full of violence and hateful voices or she was dropped off at Grandma's in the middle of the night because it had become too dangerous for her at home.

"Still, I was always happy when Ma came to get me," Erica had told me the night before. "I thought my grandma was awful, though she did take good care of me. Do you get that, Bea? Kids are strange. I still would've rather been at home."

I spent the rest of the day wandering the city and thinking about Erica, the stories from her childhood, her teenage years. Despite my desperate attempts to suppress the memory, I kept reliving the moments before her outburst, when I'd given in and let her take me into her arms. Why hadn't I made it clear that I didn't want that love? Why didn't I jump out of bed right away? Every time that thought came to mind, I sought salvation in the stories that came afterward. I'd come to terms with myself later, at that moment I couldn't, I didn't want to.

At five-thirty, I found myself standing in front of the newspaper offices. From the other side of the street, I gazed up at the modern façade, an unrelenting wall of translucent glass behind which I knew Erica was sitting. It was the same way I'd stood across the street from the hotel in Paris. Was this how I'd recognize the milestones of my life? With the last bit of willpower I had left, I tore myself away from that spot and sprinted toward the station. I ran away and hid in Egmond. The next day, I sent a letter of resignation to my job, citing health reasons.

Around the middle of the month, I slept with the young painter a few times after running into him on one of my walks on the beach. It was absurd—all I can say is I was trying to regain my balance.

After three weeks, I was nearly out of money and was forced to think constructively. I sent out letters of application and soon found myself having to explain myself at job interviews in Amsterdam. I was hired at an accounting firm and, ironically enough, still managed to move up in salary. It was a small office in Amsterdam South, so I could easily avoid the city center and running into Erica. I kept my desire to see her under control. My life was travel, work, travel, sleep. I was on my own and told myself that I liked it better that way.

Shortly before Christmas, I decided to take a later train home so I could do a bit of shopping in the city for a Christmas party my new colleagues were organizing. It wasn't by chance that I happened to walk by the newspaper around five-thirty. I wasn't trying to fool myself; I was simply counting on fate to respect my weakness. I didn't run into Erica there. A half-hour later, however, on the bustling Kalverstraat, she walked up to me with her bike. The first thing I noticed was that she was wearing a hat, a felt hat, like the ones men wear, with a little dip in the top. Then I saw, in the shadow of the pulled-down brim, that one side of her face was swollen, and her eye was embedded in a dark shade of purple and green. She was limping a bit, too. The smile she'd tried to give me seemed painful for her, and she retracted it into a comical grin.

"Did you fall?" I asked. Her rough state made things a bit easier for me in that moment. She gave me a meaningful look followed by that half-cheerful grimace.

"Dolly's a little sadistic," she said in an attempt to shock me.

The ostentation of the statement caught me off guard.

"Really." I said, hoping that the one-word answer would come off as both sarcastic and neutral.

She slipped her free arm through mine and pulled me close.

"Let's go have a cup of tea," she commanded warmly and gave my arm a pinch. "No excuses, the last train isn't leaving for a while." She'd thus assumed I had stayed in Egmond, or maybe she was keeping tabs on me. We sat across from each other at a café table and Erica, loud and in good spirits, ordered an assortment of pastries, which was placed between us.

"Here, custard for you," she whisked a cream puff onto my plate. "Or would you rather have a croquette, *Mademoiselle . . .*" she roared.

"No, this is fine." Only then did my heart start pounding and the emotions hit me. But I had to save what was left to be saved. I looked at my watch.

"I still want to catch the seven o'clock train. Someone's coming over tonight."

"Cut the act," Erica said. "When are you coming home?"

Home. Where was that? On the Prinsengracht? Or with her, wherever she happened to be living?

"Never," I said. In my desperate attempt to sound firm, the word came out so shrill that the people at the next table looked over at us.

Erica laughed. "Shhh . . . no need to shout it from the rooftops, now."

She wolfed down the pastries with pleasure, but I couldn't help but notice her hand tapping nervously on the table, the way she avoided my gaze, the drops of sweat forming on her forehead, that she was also unsettled by our encounter.

"It's too hot in here," she said irritably as she pulled off her coat and hung it over the chair. "Well, now's your chance," she continued. "I'm about to move again. Dolly pushed me down the stairs." She pointed to her eye. "That's the third time she's attacked me. I'm crazy about her, but enough is enough."

I made a motion to stand. I couldn't tolerate the vulgarity of her life and the arrogant way she talked about it. I felt dizzy and nauseous and needed fresh air. What had those few weeks since our separation done to her? When I got up, she grabbed me by the wrist, and forced me back down into my chair with her small, strong hand. She was as white as a sheet and the contrast with her black eye was disconcerting.

"Admit it, Bea," she said. They were the same words she'd said to me that night, but this time there was no triumph, no drive in her voice. I knew I would succumb to her insistence, to the supplication in her tear-filled eyes, her treacherously trembling mouth.

I tore myself away from her, fled from the café and into the street. I ran all the way to the station, unable to control my sobs.

That evening I wrote her a long letter. I took three bromide tablets so I wouldn't get emotional and would be able to tell her matter-of-factly that I belonged to a different world than she did. Paper is patient—that's what they'd always told me when I was a girl.

The next morning on the train, I tore the pages to shreds and let them flutter out the window. It offered momentary relief, but all I'd done was rinse away the bubbling, foaming surface; I didn't dare disturb the dark craters of my soul. I'd simply bought myself peace of mind by ignoring who I was. Because of my attitude—which I myself didn't understand at the time, but which stemmed from the decision that Erica and

I inhabited two different worlds—she never tried to squeeze my real feelings out of me again. She, too, understood that I'd closed the gates and taken refuge on the other side of the border, safe behind the barbed-wire fencing I'd put up around myself. She accepted the consequences and respected my decision. I went to the devil one last time to confess, but after this "slip-up" I was healed forever.

Our reconciliation came as a result of the war, which ultimately penetrated my self-imposed isolation. I started to worry about Erica's safety. First of all, she was half-Jewish. I'd overheard a lot of conversations among my Jewish colleagues and was thus able to see through the delusions of most Dutch Jews, who had too much faith in their country to fear Hitler's racist insanity. The accountant I worked for was Jewish and so were most of his clients; the bookkeeper and I were the only gentiles on staff. This environment opened me up to new perspectives, and naturally Erica was at the center of my new worldview. I also thought of Van der Lelie, whose tactics I'd feared since the night Erica confessed. My boss had told me all about the paper's political views, and he didn't mince words. The only reason he kept getting the newspaper was to stay up to date on Nazi sentiments in the Netherlands, and you could read a lot between the lines. Just like when Erica was in France, I was tortured by the thought of what might happen to her. This time, my concern offered no pretext for my desire. My anxiety was real and stronger than my own self-interest. I wrote her another letter, which I planned to send to her to at the paper, but when I read through it, it seemed overly alarmist: What are your plans? Don't you know how dangerous it is? I ripped it up and wrote another one in which I insisted we meet for special reasons. She called me at the office and suggested a bar where we could meet. Remembering how our last meeting went, I invited her to Egmond on Saturday afternoon instead. This hadn't been my intention, but when I heard that familiar presumption in her voice, I imagined another scene and decided it was better not to meet in public. We agreed to meet at Central Station at one-thirty.

That Saturday, I waited at the station for her for an hour and eventually went home, where I waited for several hours more. She finally showed up around dinner time. Of course, I was so annoyed from all the waiting by then, and all the indignation, doubt, disgust, and regret that came with it, that my carefully prepared speech degenerated into an accusation . . . Was she just sitting around waiting for the Germans to invade? Was she completely incapable of facing reality? Did she think the Krauts were going to make a detour to save Holland? Did she really think that the Dutch Jews—or half-Jews for that matter—would be treated any differently than the ones in Poland and Germany? Didn't she know that the director of the newspaper was a known Nazi? And his crony, Mr. Van der Lelie? As if she could count on him for protection! If I were her, I'd be packing my bags. More important people than she had already left the country.

Erica seemed flattered by my aggressive speech, my concern. She clung to every word and behind her eyes was a look of barely hidden amusement, of victory. I realized that I'd exposed myself, that now Erica knew what was going on inside me. And I knew it too. There was no turning back. When she put her arms around me and pulled my rigid body into her chest, I let her do it. We stood there for a long time until she whispered something in my ear. I couldn't make out what she said, and she had to repeat it. She never spoke those few words again. It wasn't necessary. We both knew they were irrevocable and would last forever. We've accepted it, each in our own way.

After Erica had left on the last bus, I slowly walked home. It was now up to me to help her get out of the country. The most obvious option was off the table. Erica had all of one hundred guilders in her savings account, which I was still keeping for her. I hadn't been able to put aside any savings since I'd gone back to work. As far as I could tell, there were two options, and I didn't know which one seemed worse, Pa or Judy. And I knew that a loan from Erica's father would undoubtedly lead to a reunion with Judy anyway. She would have to send Erica's emigration papers. So, we decided on America. There was no point in staying in Europe, and Erica had no interest in the Dutch East Indies. Judy—yes, Judy—had lured her across the pond. Her name wasn't mentioned during our deliberations, but I knew it as if Erica had made me a partner in her secret hope. She avoided my gaze whenever I mentioned the United States as the best solution and reacted with too much indifference. Moreover, we didn't know anyone else who could foot the bill. We both knew it without having to say it out loud. And so what? Erica was leaving, I was staying behind. During those days of endless pondering and deliberation, I kept hitting the same dead end, where I'd come to the conclusion that my plan would never work. Erica would just have to stay here, god damn it, we'd have to risk it. And she wasn't the only one. There were thousands of others in the same position who couldn't leave either. Maybe the imminent danger would all blow over. And if it got to that point, we could always plot an escape later on. But I'd lost faith in the honesty of my contemplations. No, I couldn't even give my secret feelings a chance. Every time, I hastily returned to the cycle of my thoughts.

"Pa!" Erica said when I presented her with my solution. She found the proposition so amusing that she started giggling and saying his name over and over again in different tones. But finally she came to a decision, slapped her knee and said: "All right, let's do it. Why not?"

I waited for news about the outcome of her mission in a café across from the newspaper offices. She returned within my estimated timeframe, and I could tell right away that she'd received more than a simple rejection. Without a word, she collapsed into a chair next to mine.

"Well?" I asked, but she didn't answer.

After a long silence she said with a contorted smile, "Did I ever tell you that Dolly and I went to a fortune-teller not too long ago?"

When she saw that I was surprised and a little irritated, she quickly added: "It was just for fun of course, in a crazy mood, but Dolly . . . anyway . . . the lady said I was exceptionally musical and should learn to play the violin." She smiled sarcastically. "Now I get it. You may as well know, Bea, my father was a Polish violinist." She stopped there. I took one look at her face and called for the check, then I led her out of the bar as soon as possible. Out on the street, I put my arm around her shoulders. We walked slowly, and I waited patiently for an explanation. Every now and then, I gave her shoulder an encouraging pinch. When my gentle "just tell me what happened" didn't help either, I left it at that. In the end, I got tired of wandering around aimlessly and decided to force the issue.

"So your father was a Polish violinist," I said as lightly as possible. Apparently, I'd hit the right note. The statement was so matter of fact that it sounded absurd. Suddenly, we both started laughing, Erica nervously, uncontrollably. Then the whole story came out. Pa had refused Erica's request for a loan. She'd called him out, said that she was his daughter and that he hadn't done anything for her since he left her mother. Even he had to admit that she'd never asked him for anything before. He flew into a rage and, as the staff pricked their ears in the next room, he shouted that she was *not* his daughter. Sparing no details, he went on to paint a complete portrait of her mother, "that whore." Erica fled the scene and had to pass through the office on her way out—the entire staff was staring. She really emphasized this last detail.

"What does he do for a living?" I asked, trying to distract her.

"Pa is . . ." She stopped short, realizing that Pa was the wrong word. "He's an importer," she corrected herself.

"I still think Pa is a good name for him," I said, "You've always said it in a mocking tone."

"Well, Pa, then," she yielded. She slipped her arm through mine, and we picked up the pace. I had helped her for a moment, but when we said goodbye after dinner, I could tell by her posture and the way she hung her head that she hadn't fully recovered from the blow.

After a sleepless night, during which I found myself identifying with Erica's feelings, I called her at the newspaper early the next morning. She wasn't there. I tried to track her down, which was ridiculous, because I didn't even know Dolly's last name. I waited for a message from her for two weeks and called the newspaper several times, but they hadn't heard from her either. In my desperation, I even asked to speak to Van der Lelie. He didn't come to the phone but relayed the message that Miss Boekman was no longer a member of the newspaper's staff.

9

In the end, it was Dolly of all people who called. She didn't seem nearly as haughty as she was the day I met her.

"Can you come?" she asked. "I can't take her anymore, and she's really gone off the deep end."

I left work and hurried over to the address she'd given me on the Achterburgwallen. It was one of those dilapidated canal houses that would probably be condemned nowadays but which, as long as they went unnoticed by the housing department and didn't accidently cave in on themselves, seemed to attract artistic types and people who were as unstable as the houses themselves. Truly hardworking artists, I thought, with the pedantry needed to boost my own self-confidence, lived in stable houses, where they could carry out their work without constantly having to deal with structural decay. The house was so crooked that I wanted to reach across it with outstretched arms and pull it straight.

I searched for a nameplate above the crumbling front steps, but there was none. Since no one answered the doorbell and the door was slightly ajar, I presumed I could just walk in. The hall was dark and cold. According to Dolly's directions, I had to go up to the top floor, so I felt my way up the dark stairwell. Above me, I could hear someone playing a waltz on the piano and the shuffling of feet.

"Dolly!" I cried in desperation. It felt like a ridiculous thing to do, but suddenly the waltz stopped.

"Dolly, there's somebody in the hall," a man yelled, and the door was opened by a girl in a bathing suit.

I entered a long, empty room, a kind of studio with mirrors and a bar along one of the walls, a bed, a piano, a cabinet, and a trapeze in the corner. The young man at the piano looked at me indifferently for a moment, and in the middle of the room were a few girls eyeing me with curiosity. Dolly came over. So, she was a dancer. I'd never asked what she did for a living, but it made sense. I didn't know anything about dancers back then, and I have to admit that I looked down on the profession. Frankly, the idea that someone would want to jump around on stage and twist themselves into every possible position filled me with suspicion. Dolly's skimpy leotard and her unnaturally long, muscular legs sticking out at the groin didn't put me at ease either. I looked up at her with a lost expression on my face, into her cold, blue eyes, at the rosy-white forehead above them, at all the unfathomable thoughts wandering around behind it. With a gesture of impatience, she tucked her sweaty, red hair behind her ears. What was I supposed to say? What did she want from me? She walked toward another door at the end of the room.

"She's in here," she said, as if she were referring to a sick dog.

The small room—Erica's sanctuary, I concluded—was dark and filthy. That much was clear. The door closed behind me, and the waltz resumed at Dolly's command. There, under the window, on a low, wide couch that consumed most of the tiny

DOLA DE JONG

room, was Erica, lying with her face in the pillow. The blanket had slipped halfway off her, and I saw that she was fully dressed.

Can I describe the rest of that afternoon? How it wasn't until I was feverishly scrubbing and cleaning that it dawned on me that Erica was sleeping off her drunkenness? All the repulsive details that revealed the kind of life she'd been leading? Her hat and coat lying in vomit on the floor, the moldy plates and glasses in the sink, the filthy clothes, empty bottles, overflowing ashtrays, old newspapers, the rotten food all over the place? I hadn't known that a human being could fall into such a state. And as I stubbornly cleaned, the rehearsal in the studio next door continued. Erica had suffered alone with the sound of dancing feet and mechanical music ringing in her ears. There had been people close enough to hear her, but she hadn't asked for help and no one had offered any.

I listened to the music outside and waited for an interlude between two lessons to take out the trash. It took a lot of courage to ask Dolly where to go, to let her in on what I was doing. Under her indifferent gaze, I felt like an overzealous Florence Nightingale, a ludicrous saint. I asked for clean bed linen. She didn't have any at the moment, and besides, what for? The same thing would happen all over again the next day. There was no criticism, no indignation in her eyes, she just shrugged. So, I hurried out of the house and ran to the Damstraat, where I bought bed sheets, towels, underwear, and pajamas.

Erica didn't even wake up when I rolled her over to change her clothes. I washed her carefully, working around her many bruises, and wrestled the new pajamas onto her lifeless body.

"Dolly's a little sadistic"—the words played over and over again in my mind like a chorus. It was evening by the time her coat and hat were washed and hung up to dry. The dance rehearsal was over, and Dolly had gone out. Once again, I ventured out into the street to get some coffee, bread, butter, and cheese. I made my supper in the dirty kitchen.

When Erica finally woke at eleven o'clock, I was standing at her bedside with a couple of aspirins and a cup of coffee. She greeted me with an ironic smile and after scanning the room, said in the mocking tone I'd been afraid of: "Hello, Florence Nightingale!"

I stayed with her that night. The next morning, she let me take her to Egmond without protest. She was quiet the entire train ride. The only thing she said, and with that eternal derision in her voice (which may have been directed at herself), was, "Well, at least Dolly saved on the cleaning lady."

I turned toward the window, but out of the corner of my eye I saw her eyelids squeeze shut against the rising tears.

Under my care, which I tried to administer as unobtrusively as possible, she made a noticeable recovery, and I knew from experience that this would open up a new chapter in her life. She'd been denied her birthright, but I foresaw that, despite the wound she'd suffered, she would graft a new branch and quickly nourish it to full bloom, which would hide the scar for the time being. She started talking about America with determination. And I, having witnessed all the anxiety and doubt of my Jewish colleagues, encouraged her in her decision.

Then one morning, my boss disrupted the staff's lethargy on the issue when he summoned us to his office and announced that he had sold the company and was leaving for America. I could feel the shame in his voice. As a Jewish man of wealth, he had the money to get out in time. Surely, he felt conscience-stricken and even a little ashamed toward his employees who were facing the same danger he was but couldn't afford to leave. Of course, he felt more Dutch than Jewish, and his decision, which was quite sensible in my opinion, left him feeling guilty. He tried to absolve himself by reminding everyone of the danger. He made quite a speech. First, he summarized the political situation, then he provided an overview of the methods the Dutch Nazi Party was using and compared its positions to those in Germany, arriving at the conclusion that the Dutch Jews were doomed to the same fate as those under Hitler. He took a book from his desk and asked the bookkeeper to pass it around. Eventually it ended up in my hands. It recounted, with endless details and statistics, the misery of the Jews under the Nazi regime. According to the Nazi ideology, Erica would be labeled "Bastard Jew I" and would likely suffer the same fate as the "real" Jews.

In addition to all the stress brought on by the sale of the business and the director's impending departure, the atmosphere at the office was incredibly tense. Work was interrupted by constant arguments among the staff. Some people thought the boss was a coward and a sellout, others were jealous and despised him for leaving. No one appreciated him for his insight. Although he'd disturbed their peace of mind, they couldn't bring themselves to admit that he was right. They were still Dutch citizens after all, and they weren't ready to relinquish the sense of security that came with it.

I took my boss's book home for Erica to look at. She put on a cool front to hide her horror, but her reaction pierced my soul.

"It's crazy, Bea! Now I'm suddenly a Jewess." She shook her head in disbelief and half-amused despair. "Life's just full of surprises," she said with a laugh. "America, America, here I come!" There was comical intonation in her voice. Truth be told, I knew she wouldn't have even considered leaving if her personal situation hadn't forced her to make a complete change.

Before the end of the week, we wrote a letter to Judy, which she asked me to sign.

"It's always better if someone else asks," Erica argued.

Right before I signed my name, something occurred to me.

"Maybe your real father wasn't even Jewish." I blurted it out without thinking. We hadn't touched on the subject again, and I was shocked by my faux pas. But still, it was a valid point and needed to be said.

"You'll have to ask Ma," she replied without hesitation.

"Me?"

"Of course, who else? It was your idea—you didn't think I'd ever want to see her again, did you?"

"But I can't . . . How could I ever ask her that, Erica? I couldn't. I'm just an outsider here. She'll shut the door in my face."

But the idea of holding Ma accountable for her sin had taken hold. Erica was not to be deterred, and in the end, I reluctantly gave in.

My conversation with Ma in the General's elegantly furnished living room might as well have been recorded on a gramophone record—I can still replay it word for word in my mind, and the painful sensation I'd felt still comes flooding back. At first, it was jovial reception, lots of "dears" and "darlings," but the warmth soon faded as my nervousness revealed that I wasn't just dropping by. I stammered through an explanation of the reason for my visit and then came the big question, which could be asked in no uncertain terms. Ma launched into a passionate monologue with a dramatic description of her living conditions in those years, followed by the plea of a condemned woman. I didn't like playing the role of prosecutor. Her emotional defense almost made me feel guilty. She wrung her hands, then dramatically pressed them against her heart and reached out to me in desperation. All of her "he" this and "he" that (in reference to her lawfully wedded husband) would've caused an executioner to doubt. I hadn't come for justice, and I tried to make this clear to her. But she wasn't listening. No matter how many times I said, "Ma, really, it's none of my business, I just wanted . . ." it just went in one ear and out the other.

Finally, her materialism got the last word.

"And why do you think I gave her my money, the only pennies anyone's ever tossed into my lap? I inherited those three thousand guilders from Jan—that was her real father's name," she added hastily, "he died and left that money to me." She started to sob. "I never saw him again, but he hadn't forgotten me."

So, the mystery of Erica's inheritance was solved. It wasn't her uncle who'd left her the three thousand guilders but her father. Erica was right—there was something fishy about that money. I remembered how strange she'd acted after she received it. She'd also alluded to it the night she confessed—penance money, she'd called it—as she was telling me about her miserable childhood and her mother's endless lecturing. Ma's affairs had taken place right under Erica's nose. As a teenager, she'd had her suspicions, but she didn't know exactly what was going on until one night when she found her mother with someone in her bed. After that, she was sent to a convent school, "cleared out of the way," as she put it, "to pay atonement for her mother's sins." As Erica told me the story, I could feel the misery of the sixteen-year-old girl who, having just discovered her mother's eroticism in a catastrophic way, was dragged away from her blissful world at the all-girls' school and locked up in the abnormal religious world of the convent.

As I listened to her mother relive her past sins, my compassion for her turned to disgust. I got up to leave. Ma began to powder her nose. There was an oppressive silence; we avoided each other's gaze. With one hand on the door, I said (and it struck me how cold and cruel my voice sounded): "I just came to ask if her father was Jewish."

Ma whipped around in fury. Her face blotchy from crying, she narrowed her eyes viciously.

"If that girl is so worried about saving her own skin, she should go ask the man herself!" she sneered. "If he even knows! He certainly did his best to figure it all out back then. A sly coward—that's what he is. He gave me his word that Erica would never . . . that filthy traitor! That's what you get from a Jew. You know, Hitler's right . . ." I didn't wait for the rest. I could still hear her carrying on in the hall. It made me dizzy. In the sober neon light of the friendly, affluent Minervalaan, where the first green of spring was sprouting in the trees and the city gardeners were preparing the lawns for flowers, the whole visit seemed so unlikely. I shook my head to wake up from the nightmare, and as I did my thoughts latched onto an old memory, one that may have surfaced to give me direction, to help me reconnect with the old Bea, with my original self. Perhaps it brought with it the realization that, through me, Erica had said goodbye to her mother for good.

It was the memory of the day my mother was buried with the lifeless baby boy who had caused her death. I remembered being in the nursery, looking through the closed curtains, their floral pattern unusually lit by the sun, at the black carriages on the street. The kitchen maid whose care I'd been entrusted to had forgotten about me. She was crying with her face in her hands. I was too young to understand what was going on, and I was curious about the commotion downstairs in front of the gate. The door swung open and my father and grandparents hurried into the room. I was lifted up and smothered with hugs and kisses. For the first and only time in my childhood, I tasted the salt of grown-up tears. For a few moments, the little girl was brought into the family circle. As small as she was, the adults needed her before making the difficult journey to the cemetery. Suddenly, my grandmother realized that she was needed more at home than at her daughter's graveside. It was a tremendous sacrifice that she was willing to make. She stayed behind at the house and played with me until the black carriages returned. It was the memory of a memory, one that has stayed with me all those years. Only then, at the age of twenty-eight, did I understand what my grandmother had felt during those hours, as she'd helped me dress and undress my dolls, cheerfully pretending, entering the imaginary world of a little girl imitating her mother, pampering and scolding her porcelain friends. She'd had to listen to that, while her daughter was being buried.

Memories from my childhood are scarce. Nothing remains from the years after my mother's death to my high school years. Recently, I found myself having to do some calculations when someone here in America asked me how old I was when my mother died. Her death left a gaping hole in my youth. Still, I'd always kept an image of her, and later as I got older my father's stories about her took on a heavenly form. How different it must have been for Erica! Instead of a guardian angel, she'd had a mother in the flesh and blood who reminded her of all the misery she'd caused.

At exactly two o'clock, the operator announced a call from Egmond. It was Erica, calling as planned.

"Well . . . ? What did she say?" She asked nervously.

"It was a waste of time," I had to be careful because I wasn't sure if the line was tapped. "She wouldn't say. Said you should just ask him."

"Oh yeah?" she said threateningly. Then there was silence.

"You still there?" I asked.

"Yes," she said, which was again followed by nothing but the crackling of the connection. But behind the silence was hate, a hate so powerful in its own powerlessness that I could almost hear it.

"See you later," she said dryly and hung up.

I went home that night full of apprehension, but Erica didn't ask me any more questions. She gave me a two-word thank you for my trouble, and I was relieved not to have to relay the entire conversation with Ma. After dinner, Erica laid the letter to Judy in front of me and asked me again to sign it. We took the epistle to the mailbox together. Before I dropped it into the slot, I looked at Erica.

"Come on," she said, "you old nag."

After that, all we could do was wait for a reply. One week later, it was the first thing I asked when I came home from work. Pretty soon, Erica couldn't take it anymore and told me to stop asking. She'd let me know. In the meantime, she ordered me to gather information from the American consulate and the shipping line. She did nothing to prepare for her departure herself. For the next two weeks, I came home to her lying on her bed reading one of the books I'd given her, the gramophone or the Dutch radio playing in the background. After a while, the bird took flight again, and I started coming home to notes in my room. "Went to the movies" or "Gone to Amsterdam." It was unusually courteous of her, and she kept it up for a little while—"Not sleeping here tonight"—but eventually there were no notes anymore, and she was gone a lot.

One morning, when I brought her breakfast in bed (something I'd started doing back when she needed it and kept doing when she slept at home), she said: "I might as well tell you— you know everything now anyway. I'm in love again. She's a cellist in the women's orchestra that's playing at the beer hall. You should come hear her sometime. She's fantastic."

Thus, she made me a partner in her escapades and in doing so, also made it easy for me to keep my distance. Without realizing it, we'd entered a new phase in our relationship.

That afternoon after work, I visited the bar in the city center where Erica had lost her heart. It was an unusually assertive move on my part. Standing nervously by the revolving door, I took a moment to find my bearings. I wondered how on earth Erica had ended up at such a kitschy German bar. I would've never even considered such a place; the patrons were from another planet. A waiter noticed me helplessly searching for someone. After my stuttering description of Erica, he sized me up from head to toe and with a cheeky smile and a wink to his co-worker directed me toward the stage. I found Erica at a table, practically at the cellist's feet. She was absorbed in her new flame and barely looked up when I, sweating all over, sat down beside her. Still, the smile on her face was for me.

"What do you think of her?" she said without turning toward me.

What do you think of her? Now that I was in on her secret, my opinion was apparently appreciated. There was no way I could tell her that I'd always found women with cellos between their knees unattractive. My father, like so many middle-class Dutch people, had been a lover of classical music, and he used to take me to concerts. One of them had featured a female cellist, and I did not enjoy it. Watching the musician, all dressed up for the occasion with a plunging décolleté to accentuate her fragility, wield the cumbersome instrument between her thighs had been confusing to me, and I'd found myself unable to appreciate her art. Afterward, I got into a fight about it with my father, who thought I was overreacting.

But the subject of Erica's interest made a better impression on me, and my expectations were a bit lower in the bierstube.

She was more enthusiastic than devoted. She played freely, in a way that was almost rough, as if ready to throw all caution to the wind.

Days later, when Inge (that was her name) played for us in Egmond, I discovered that she was incredibly talented, a true artist heart and soul. Hunched over her instrument in Erica's room, her sleek dark hair falling down over her cameo face, she was a completely different woman from the one I'd seen in the smoky bar. There, she played for money, a concession that didn't bother her because she had created another self that no one could touch. At our house, she released that other self and played like a woman possessed. It didn't even bother me that she stayed over once a week. I cared for her like I cared for Erica. The one thing that did bother me at first was the fact that she was German. Even then, people knew that Germans weren't being allowed to leave Germany, unless of course they were spies. There were a lot of rumors flying around about German tourists, and although some members of the population wrote them off as exaggerations, I couldn't rule out the possibility. Artists were only allowed to travel under the auspices of Joseph Goebbels, the Nazi minister of propaganda—that much was clear. Inge's orchestra was there to create cultural propaganda for the Third Reich, but it was also possible that their assignment extended beyond the four walls of the bierstube. My suspicions were soon dispelled. Inge proved her trustworthiness by speaking openly about the situation in Germany. She went on and on, her delicate, heart-shaped face taut with anger and rage, until we were fully convinced of her hatred for the regime. They left you no choice, she said. You did what you had to do to survive. But a few members of the orchestra actually were Nazis, and, she whispered with an anxious glance over her shoulder, they were paid more because they did other work on the side. She didn't tell us what exactly these side jobs consisted of, but it was clear enough. Her pale face whitened even more as she warned us: things would go wrong. Germany had its eye on Holland.

Erica started whistling a little tune and got up to put a record on the gramophone. It was a tic of hers that I knew well by then. My heart started pounding in my throat. We were still waiting for Judy's reply. Even if she said yes and supplied the necessary funds, it was unlikely that Erica would go at this point. I had no more illusions. Inge was more important to Erica than her desire for change or self-preservation. And time was running out. It was already early April.

When I went to the American consulate (without telling anyone) to see if there might be a message for Erica, there were long lines of Jews. The shipping company where I'd reserved a passage for Erica on good faith was now demanding payment. I had already been planning on borrowing money to cover the costs. It was up me to take care of it. Erica could no longer be bothered.

But now, standing by the gramophone, she blurted out, "*Ich bin halb Jude.*" I'm half-Jewish. She spun around to see how Inge would react. I was suddenly aware that there was some kind of drama going on between them. Erica didn't care about the danger, she just wanted to know how much Inge had been influenced by racist theories, and whether or not her feelings for Erica could withstand Hitler's ideology. In spite of myself, I felt sorry for Inge.

"That's not possible," Inge said, ready to scold Erica for making such an off-color joke. But Erica pierced her with her eyes and didn't let her go, betraying nothing. Inge looked to me for help. I'll never forget how uneasy I felt in that moment. All I could do was nod in agreement.

"But then . . ." Inge began, "then . . ." She jumped up and looked wildly from Erica to me, searching for the right words to adequately express her horror. "But then there's no time to lose!" She fixed her eyes desperately on me. "What are you going to do? What are we going to do?"

She sank back down in the chair. In a few steps, Erica was behind her with her face pressed against hers. I got up and collected the dirty ashtrays. As I emptied them, I heard Erica whispering into Inge's ear. She'd passed the test, I thought bitterly. Maybe deep down I was hoping that Inge would react differently. Who knows? Maybe I'd become overly suspicious, maybe I was trying to get too deeply involved.

After a wave of inexplicable bitterness, I concluded that Erica had come to terms with her own illegitimacy. Her father had officially recognized her as his child, so it was on her record. Rather than calling her Ma to account or interrogating Pa further, she simply resigned herself to the situation.

10

BY THE END OF APRIL, I gave up waiting. Apparently, the whole thing with Judy was over, and I blamed myself for not taking Erica more seriously when she'd said, "For Judy, those kinds of things are more of an adventure. She can take it or leave it." No wonder Erica didn't talk about it! She must've been hurt by Judy's abandonment. Or else that too had left her cold. There was nothing and no one else in the world to her but Inge. Erica's love life replaced all logic. That's how it had been with Dolly and Judy, and that's how it was again. And I had to admit that I, too, had been her main subject of interest once, albeit with less *preponderance*.

I plodded on at the office and worked overtime, which I was paid extra for. We needed the money. I was working for two now. Erica was borrowing from me on a regular basis—she always said, "I'll make it up to you later." The remainder of Ma's inheritance was still in her savings account. She didn't ask about it, and I didn't dare bring it up. We both just "forgot" about it. As far as I know, it's still in there. Every now and then, I take out the book and hold it in my hands. It's always traveled with my other papers and turned yellow over the years.

Once again, I found myself living largely alone. In the evening, I took my work home with me. It was a welcome distraction, and I took great satisfaction in carrying out the tasks my boss had entrusted to me in preparation for his departure. In all my brooding loneliness, his appreciation was a comfort. It was a cordial goodbye. He said he would never forget me, "You were the best secretary I ever could've asked for, if you ever need any help . . ." At that moment, neither of us expected me to actually take him up on those words, but I've been his secretary in New York for years. He helped me out tremendously when I wanted to leave Holland after the war. But that's getting off the subject. When the new director took over the accounting firm in Amsterdam, I got along with him too. At the office, I'm always the best version of myself.

I resigned myself to wait and see what happened. I was amazed by the fatalism that had gripped the population, but it also brought me a certain sense of anxiety. Maybe it would all work itself out. Who knows, maybe I'd gotten carried away with all my worrying about Erica. Even my colleagues at the office calmed down after the boss left. Not being constantly reminded of the danger seemed to come as a relief. The new owner became the main subject of discussion.

Erica and Inge spent the night in Egmond once a week. I lived for those evenings, when they'd let me into the sanctuary of their union. I didn't know what Erica did in Amsterdam. All she told me was that she spent her evenings at the bierstube and then went back with Inge to her guesthouse. So, she spent night after night sitting in a bar at Inge's feet? How could she stand it? I thought back on the waiter's suggestive little smile and shuddered.

Then came the blow, at least for Erica, and in a way for me as well because I drew my conclusions from it. On May 4, the women's orchestra ended its engagement and left for Germany. Erica showed up unexpectedly at the house that night, defeated.

"Didn't Inge know this was coming?" I asked innocently. Erica shrugged.

"Of course, but she didn't want to say goodbye."

"Come on!" I said. "You don't really believe that!"

She didn't respond and disappeared into her room. In the middle of the night, however, she came in and sat on my bed. She was still fully dressed and in a frantic state, as if she needed to get something off her chest. At first, she talked about Inge. In her misery, she told me all kinds of things they did together that I didn't want to know and were painful to hear.

"She knew," she finally said. "She'd known for a week. The orchestra was supposed to stay until the end of the month and then play in Rotterdam. That was the official plan. But last week she heard they'd been called back. They weren't allowed to talk about it. She didn't dare tell me. It was top secret and too dangerous to discuss. Even with me. She didn't trust any of the others. She was afraid my reaction would attract attention."

"Well that says a lot," I said alarmed. "If they're calling Germans back to Germany . . ." I didn't finish the sentence. Erica dug into in her skirt pocket, pulled out a crumpled envelope and handed it to me. It had an American stamp on it and had been sent via registered mail.

"I lied to you," Erica confessed. "She wrote back within a week. I already spent the money."

The images of the following period have replayed in my mind hundreds of times, and now, thirteen years later, the details have consolidated into a single memory. All it takes is a single glance for the feelings to come rushing back, to know that, despite the agonizing pain of losing Erica, she depended on me for half a year, and, as much as I could allow it, had been mine.

What came afterward, the haunting question as to why I imposed certain restrictions on our relationship, my regret over a decision that I didn't doubt for a second at the time, but that later I couldn't understand—that was the legacy of the time, a legacy that has nestled into my tissue like a tumor, harmless as long as new cells can grow around it. Sometimes, during sleepless nights, that growth takes on a life of its own, and it takes all the willpower I have to save myself, to cast off the doubt and regret and rebuild myself anew. Nothing will ever change what happened. We can't go back. On the surface I've moved on, the slate's been wiped clean, my life has continued.

But now that I am coming to terms with the most critical period of my life, the only time that really mattered, I'm compelled to take one last look at what happened during the first months of the occupation.

I now see that the shock of Erica's extreme unreliability hadn't fully hit me. I was too caught up in the strange, incomprehensible satisfaction it gave me. And then, before I had the chance to regain my balance and make one last wild attempt to help Erica flee the country, the Germans invaded.

It's too late, I thought, it's just too late. Unsurprisingly, my initial reaction to the invasion was entirely focused on Erica. In my state of mind, I considered Erica's precarious position to be more important than the disaster that had befallen our country.

I still remember how she sat by the radio for hours, feverishly tense at first, but soon utterly dismayed. It became a kind of vigil.

For me, that's where the war began, in Erica's room. The image of her leaning into the radio as if she were attached to it represented the invasion, the battles, the bombings, the defeat of a proud people. I saw only Erica, shattered, so completely paralyzed that the voice coming from the speaker was the only thing she had to hold on to.

And I could tell by the way she shook her head in disbelief that, in addition to her despair, she was staggered by her own recklessness. It was upsetting to see her like this, though deep down I felt a gnawing sense of atonement. Inside me was a smoldering flame of satisfaction that even my pity and fear couldn't extinguish.

I worked more than necessary to cover our living expenses because constant activity was the only way to escape my unbearable thoughts. But every time I came home from work or from running errands in town, where people huddled together in small groups or gazed at each other wide-eyed in the street, I found Erica as I'd left her. That's how we entered the occupation period. Erica had burned all her bridges. No work, no money, no family, no friends—she'd lost everything. She had nothing and no one but me. In an effort to bring her back to reality, I tried to talk about Inge. Where was she? Would we ever hear from her? My intentions were good, but Erica saw it differently. She shook her head furiously, as if my question had been too much for her, as if thinking about Inge would destroy her. It made we want to bite my tongue off. Even now, I shudder to think of how harsh and stupid I was, the cruelty of my mistake.

But there wasn't much time to dwell on it then. We had to make plans. Under the circumstances, we were better off living in Amsterdam. I foresaw that commuting back and forth through occupied territory would eventually become too complicated. Who knew what would happen next? We seemed better off moving back to the city on our own free will than waiting around to be evacuated with the other residents. I was pessimistic from the start, and yet, in hindsight, I was acting intuitively. I never could've imagined the misery to come. I told Erica to find us a place to live, because I had to work.

"But remember, not on the Achterburgwallen," I warned.

She responded with a long, penetrating look.

"Madame has conditions," she said sharply, "Madame is boss now."

The caustic comment saved us from a major blowout. The position of caretaker and guardian angel that I'd taken up so naturally had gone to my head. Erica saw through it. Her proud resistance brought me back down to earth, and thanks to her we were able to enter into this abnormal period in a healthy way. Despite her dependency, she remained my equal and didn't give me the chance to take the upper hand. I'm still ashamed of my momentary imperiousness, especially since I've had to suppress a tendency to dominate a number of other times since then. But it wasn't so easy for me either. My need to protect Erica didn't stand a chance against her desire for autonomy. She was so independent that it was hard to know how to help her, and she was unburdened by obligations. The concept of yours and mine was of no interest to her. In her eyes, it all came down to the uncertainty of the situation. The way she saw it, I happened to be in a more advantageous position, but if the roles had been reversed, she obviously would've taken care of me too. It was just a coincidence that the opportunity never presented itself. That's how Erica saw life and that was the philosophy I had to contend with. It was up to me to keep things in balance.

In the summer of 1940, Erica went off on her own again. Yes, she felt the significance of the bond between us and continued to call our new attic apartment home; yes, she was warm and considerate toward me, but she remained fiercely independent. She didn't have a job and she wasn't looking for one. She was too busy. I knew what she was up to as if she'd told me herself, but I played dumb. With fear in my heart, I'd wait for her to come home. Sometimes she was gone for days. It was so like her to get involved in underground activities. It was small acts of sabotage that paved the way for organized resistance. It seemed innocent at the time, and at first it didn't have much impact. I made things easy for myself and for her by not talking about it, by pretending to be naïve. I spent my days at the office, earning money for both of us. But inside me was the growing conviction that Erica wouldn't survive the war if she stayed in Holland. Apart from the persecution of the Jews (which seemed like nothing at first, but I, in my pessimism, saw it as a ticking time bomb), my knowledge of Erica's character was enough to make me worry about the other dangers she might face. To be honest, I was more worried about her actions than her ancestry. She couldn't compromise, make the best of it, and try to stay out of harm's way like the majority of the population. The circumstances of her life were too unusual for that. She had constructed her raison d'être piece by piece, and her only hope for future happiness was to challenge fate, which had always been her sworn enemy.

I had to protect Erica from herself. That's the way I saw it. Didn't I admire her initiative, her courage? Wasn't I proud of her? In a way, I was—no need to claim otherwise. At the same time, however, I realized that heroes like Erica are doomed. They're too spontaneous, too unstable. It's the heart that calls us to action—as it should be—but for the action to be successful the mind has to take over. I knew that, no matter what, Erica's heart would continue calling the shots. And so, I quietly made plans. I sold the jewelry my grandmother had left me and used the money to buy a false identification papers. I bid my time, waiting for the right moment to persuade her to leave. Meanwhile, I tried to sabotage her work. It's true. I kept her from her dangerous activities by assigning her the time-consuming task of collecting our rations. And Erica, in an effort to do her part for our household, stood in line for hours. At the end of the summer, when she still refused to flee and told me there was no point pursuing the matter any further, I went so far as to fake a nervous breakdown and kept her at my bedside for three weeks. I'm not ashamed of it. I had one goal, to protect Erica. Didn't I have the right to try? Eventually, the underground movement replaced her. Call me selfish, call me immoral, I don't care. I did what I had to do and had no qualms about it.

In November, we received a surprise visit from Ma, *the Comrade!*

I was home alone, and her unexpected visit sent me into a panic. Please God let her be gone before Erica comes home, I thought. It was still an hour before dinner, but she might be early. The odds were slim, but there was a chance.

I was almost rude to Ma. I said I was extremely surprised to see her, didn't invite her in, pretended to be in a hurry, said I was right in the middle of cooking and that Erica generally didn't come home for dinner. But she followed me up to the kitchen and made easy work of climbing the stairs.

She was wearing the uniform of the National Socialist Women's Organization. The girlish-looking suit, with the little hat perched sideways on top of her overly long black hair, looked ridiculous on her. Her cheeks were covered in rouge and her lips had a bluish tint to them. The dark lines along her eyebrows and eyelashes accentuated her flaxen, wrinkled skin. But she was lively and quick to tell me how her role as group leader made her feel young again, how it had enriched her life. She made a great effort to convince me of the importance of her position and convey just how indispensable she was to the cause. I listened tacitly while my thoughts jumped back and forth between repulsion and pity and other calculations.

But my desire to avoid a meeting between Erica and Ma took precedent. In a last-ditch effort to get her out of the house, I suggested that we go out for a drink, "You know, at that cozy bar around the corner?" I didn't have any alcohol in the house and hated to see her go dry, I said. But it was no use. Ma hadn't seen "the child" for so long; she'd deliberately chosen this time of day to drop by because she knew Erica would be home. That drink could wait.

"What are you doing here?" Erica said when she walked into the kitchen around six-thirty.

"Well, young lady . . ." Ma began. She stood up and smoothed her narrow skirt. For a moment, she gasped for words, but Erica didn't wait.

"Come on, Ma, buzz off. You've got no business here," and with a scathing glance at Ma's outfit, she added, "Nazis aren't welcome in this house." She swung open the door and nodded toward the stairs.

Apparently, Ma had been prepared for such a reception.

"I'd watch my tongue if I were you, young lady," she said. "You're a real piece of work, you know that? I know more about you than you think."

Erica sized her up and laughed scornfully. I felt the blood drain from my face. Just a few weeks before, I'd gotten my hands on a few yards of high-quality wool on the black market, and, at Erica's insistence, had a seamstress use it to make her a kind of sleeved vest and a pair of pants. I hadn't protested against the strange get-up because Erica had argued that she needed something warm to wear with all the coal rationing. The suit made her look like a teenage boy, but at least it would protect her from the cold.

"I'm going to count to thirty," Erica said. "If you're not on the stairs by then, I'll push you down them myself."

"Erica!" I cautioned, in spite of myself. But she ignored me. She'd gone deathly pale, wheezing as she began to count painfully slowly. The roles were reversed, that much was clear. I realized that Ma must have presented Erica with the same ultimatum back when she was in control, and God knows what the circumstances had been back then. It wasn't any kind of normal manifestation of parental authority.

Ma didn't make any motion for the door. She laughed defiantly, tugged down her corset in the vulgar way that fat women dressed too young for their age do, and took a few steps back. Trapped between her and the stove, I just stood there in the steam of the boiling potatoes, my legs shaking, barely able to support my weight. I never knew it could take so long to count to thirty.

"All right, Ma, Erica," I said, trying to bring things to a close.

Before I knew what was happening, Erica had grabbed me by the wrists, jerked me out of the kitchen, and pushed me so hard into my room that I tripped and slid across the floor. She slammed the door shut behind me. I just lay there, stunned by the shock and pain of my fall, and listened to the scuffle unfolding in the hall, the shuffling feet, the stumbling on the stairs, Erica's hoarse panting, Ma's screams. Then came the voice of our downstairs neighbor who'd come out to see what was going on. People on the other floors shouted for an explanation as well. The house exploded into chaos.

Finally, Erica came back upstairs and said, "Well, that's done." She wiped her hands as if she'd just finished a chore. The sober remark was accompanied by Ma's shrieking in the entry hall, curses and threats alternated with explanations to the neighbors. No one seemed to answer her. The residents in our building were all "good" people. I heard doors closing and knew that everyone had gone back to their own apartments. After a while, Ma had blown off all her steam, and I heard her footsteps heading toward the door to the street. A few seconds later, the door shut behind her. After that, Erica went into the kitchen. The sound of the pan in the sink, the murmur of water echoed through me. She drained the potatoes. As I slowly crawled to my feet, I realized with renewed shock that Erica was headed down the stairs. Moments later the door to the street closed behind her. I could feel her standing on the stoop, lighting a cigarette, her fingers trembling. Through my bedroom window, I saw her hurry across the street and disappear around the corner.

11

A FEW DAYS LATER, the Germans raided our house. They showed up around midnight and ransacked the place. I was alone. Erica hadn't come home. As I answered their questions truthfully, told them that my roommate had left, that I didn't know where she was, I thought about what our downstairs neighbor had said when she came upstairs to check on us after the fight.

"You ought to be careful, that woman's a party member . . . If she reports you . . . God—mother and daughter," she stopped short. "Things are just terrible these days," she said and went back downstairs in tears.

That night, when the Germans asked me what Erica's profession was, I said "writer." They left with a pile of notebooks that she'd filled with poetic musings as a teenager.

I stayed up until the early hours of the morning sorting the beans and peas that the Germans had poured all over the floor. I can still feel the knobby legumes between my fingers as I picked them up one by one and dropped them into the right bags; I still remember the thoughts that were released inside me and rearranged into new paradigms.

Once again, I found myself waiting at home, waiting to see what would happen next. It felt like an eternity, but in reality, the fatal message arrived within a week. Dolly came over at seven o'clock in the morning to tell me that Erica was in prison in the Weteringschans.

It was too much for me to process all at once. I was confused as to why Dolly was bringing the news, and after the sound of the doorbell at that ungodly hour had nearly given me a heart attack, the news itself felt almost anticlimactic. I remember drinking the glass of ice-cold water that Dolly had handed me and how humiliated I was to be having a nervous breakdown in front of her, of all people.

"You'll get an official message," she said matter-of-factly. "You can bring her a fresh change of clothes and things." She stood over my chair, calm and collected. Once again, I felt small and ridiculous next to her. I tried to stand, but my legs wouldn't allow it.

"Don't bother, just sit," she said. "I've got to get going. I just came to warn you. Do you have money? You won't get anywhere without money and influence. You'll hear from me."

She was already at the door when I called after her. "Dolly—" even saying her name aloud was difficult for me. I barely knew her and had never called her by her name. "Dolly, what happened? What did she do?"

"Do?" She laughed. "You really are naïve. You know Erica, don't you?"

"So, was she living . . . ?" I ventured. "How do you know? When did it happen?"

"Last night. She didn't come home, and I went out looking for her." She chuckled. "Jesus, that Erica! She didn't stand a chance, and yet . . . She'd heard about the raid from one of your neighbors in the movement. Betrayed, of course, by you know who. I'd forbidden her to . . ." She fell quiet and looked at me searchingly for a moment. Then her eyes became hard, as cold and callous as they'd been that day in the dance studio. "If you weren't such a pushover . . . God knows what she sees in you. You're neither one nor the other. Why don't you just let her go? What do you want from her? Well, it's none of my business. What is my business is getting her out. You'll hear from me."

In the end, there was nothing I could do. I tried everything, the impossible, the lowest I could think of. Dolly was my accomplice, my anchor and support. It was through her that I got in touch with the underground movement. I was referred to a lawyer in The Hague with good connections, but he wanted eight thousand guilders, which I didn't have and there absolutely no way I was going to be able to scrape it together, but I had to try. I even went to Pa to beg. He swore he didn't have the money, though I could tell he was torn.

"Logical," Dolly declared when I told her about his refusal. "He needed it for his own escape, he's gone." How did she know that? "I went to see him myself after you failed. I'm better suited to these tasks than you are. But the bird had flown the coop."

I gathered all my courage.

"Ma," I said. "Blackmail." There was that word again, it had become so familiar, so easy to say out loud. After all the days of deliberation, I'd rehearsed a dialogue with Ma over and over again in my mind. Dolly shrugged.

"You got proof? Then forget about it, darling."

Still, I tried. I'll never forget what an excruciating undertaking it was. Ma was really on her high horse.

"She's being treated very well there," she said. "It'll do her good, she needs to learn a lesson. Don't worry, she's got everything she needs. I've been sending her a package every week actually. Anonymously, of course. Before you know it, she'll be back on your doorstep. Pretty soon you'll both realize that the Germans aren't the evil ones."

I'd saved my weapon for the end, but Ma beat me to it. A few words had been enough. She already knew what I was going to say.

"Prove it," she said. "And I'd be careful if I were you. Before you know it, you'll be the one locked up. I'll tell you something else, young lady. Even if they believed you, even if you could prove it, they couldn't care less about me. Pa was a Jew, don't forget that. And if you really want the truth, Erica's father wasn't. One Jew was enough for me. Now go home and relax. Your dear friend will be home in a few weeks. Then you can . . ." I didn't let her finish, because if she'd completed that sentence, I would have attacked her and destroyed the only hope we had left.

"She's still your child, Ma," I said, nearly choking on the words.

"Yes, and I've done a lot of favors for her over the years without so much as a word of thanks. All my sacrifices for nothing. I struggled for her my entire life . . . the best upbring-ing, the finest schools . . ."

"Erica knows that, Ma. She talks about it a lot." I continued with my betrayal, after all, that's what it was. Erica could never know about this visit. But my lies had a profound effect on Ma. She became visibly milder and soon switched to the role of the misunderstood, acquiescent mother.

"Bea, you're still so young, you don't understand, child.

For a mother, there's no sacrifice too great. But if nothing comes of it, well, let me be honest with you, when your child still grows up to be so abnormal . . . God only knows how she got this way, she most certainly didn't get it from my side of the family," a coquettish smile slid across her face. "Anyway, you know what I mean. Not an ounce of gratitude, no love in return." Her eyes welled up with sentimental tears.

"Still, you don't let your own child sit in jail," I tried again. "You do have some influence in the party, don't you?"

"It'll all work out," Ma said hastily. "Don't worry about it."

Later, at Dolly's, I cried for the first time in weeks, and she showed sympathy.

"Oh, you poor little sap," she said. "What a mess! And what a stupid bitch that woman is! She honestly thinks they'll make Erica sit in the corner for a little while and then let her go."

In the end, Dolly and I were sidekicks, almost friends. I learned to appreciate her, and she stopped showing so much disdain toward me.

The weeks turned into months. Life became more difficult by the day, but most of it just passed me by. There was nothing to do but wait. Sometimes I went to Dolly's. We'd sit in front of her wood stove in silence in the room that had once belonged to Erica.

In February, there was a kind of trial where I saw Erica one last time. She smiled at us, at Dolly and me. Shortly afterward she was sent to Vught, and in April I received word that she had died. Pneumonia, according to the postcard I pulled out of the mailbox.

Greenwich Village – January 1954

Translator's Note

EVERY WRITER HAS THEIR FAVORITE WORDS. As a translator, you get to know them intimately. One of de Jong's is *koortsachtig*— feverish, frenetic. We feel that feverishness in Erica's caprices, her impulsivity, her tendency toward self-destruction. We see it in Bea's unwavering—and at times unfathomable—tolerance of Erica's behavior, her irrepressible urge to keep Erica close, and her inner battle against her own desires. Shortly after I started working on this translation, I gave the Dutch version to a my father-in-law to read. The next day he emailed me: "I read it in one breath." In an effort to preserve the pace and the vivacity of the original, this feverishness entered my translation as well.

Dola de Jong was born Dorothea Rosalie de Jong in 1911 in Arnhem, The Netherlands, to a wealthy Jewish father and a German mother, who died when de Jong was five. As a young woman, she aspired to become a ballet dancer, but her conservative father viewed ballet as "one step away from prostitution," as she told *Het Parool* in a 1982 interview. Her father wanted to send her to a finishing school in Lausanne, "but I was a rebel," she said, "I always have been." She took a job at a local newspaper and eventually moved to Amsterdam in the early 1930s where she worked as a freelance journalist and secretary. While many around her were in denial of the growing threat to the east, de Jong was quick to realize that the Netherlands was no longer safe for Jewish people. She fled the country for Tangier in April 1940, weeks before the Nazis invaded Holland. There, she married her first husband (whom she would later divorce) and started a ballet school for children. It was the father of one of her students who helped the young couple obtain the necessary papers to move to America. They settled in New York City, where de Jong would live for most of her life. Her father, stepmother, and brother stayed behind the Netherlands and did not survive the war.

The Tree and the Vine was first published in Amsterdam in 1954 as *De Thuiswacht*—literally *The Homewait*. De Jong had been living in New York City for more than a decade by then and had published numerous children's books and one critically acclaimed novel, *And the Field is the World* (*En de akker is de wereld*), which had been acquired by legendary Scribners editor Maxwell Perkins. As Eva Cossee notes, when she submitted the manuscript of her second novel to her Dutch publisher, it was immediately declared "shameless" and "unpublishable." With the help of endorsements from prominent friends, among them her then retired editor Perkins and fellow writers in exile Leo Vroman and Marnix Gijsen, the novel found its way to publication and was met with acclaim. Gijsen called it "an important and remarkable book—and not because it addresses a delicate problem with so much understanding, that's just the starting point. I'm more in awe of the finesse with which Dola de Jong sketches her two main characters." The first English translation wouldn't come out until 1961. Decades later de Jong still referred to it as "my favorite book."

I don't know whether de Jong was involved in the first translation of *The Tree and the Vine*. If she were alive today—she died in California in 2003 at the age of 92—I have a feeling that she would have had plenty to say about this new English translation. In her correspondence with editor Angèle Manteau—which is now housed in the Special Collections department of the Royal Library of the Netherlands in The Hague—de Jong often mentions the tension she feels between her first language and the language in which she has become the most at home, English. "I can still write a letter [in Dutch]," she wrote in 1982, "but as soon as I want to take the conversation a bit deeper, it all goes south. My Dutch is so dotted with English that it hardly seems like Dutch anymore."

While it's possible that de Jong's command of her first language deteriorated over time, the influence of other languages on her Dutch is present even in *The Tree and the Vine*, which she wrote in her early forties. It is one of the things that makes her style idiosyncratic and gives it the feeling of being particular to the Netherlands of the 30s and also belonging to something broader. The text is peppered with anglicisms, which tend to disappear into the English translation, as well as French words and expressions (most likely vestiges of her upper-class background and time in French-speaking Morocco) that I tried to preserve. On the one hand, this display of linguistic versatility could be regarded as the work of an old bluestocking—an insult de Jong introduced me to in Chapter 5; on the other, it could also be a strategy to keep the text intentionally ambiguous. In Chapter 10, for example, Bea admits that, like Judy and

Dolly—two of Erica's lovers, though never named as such—she too had been the focus of Erica's attention once, "albeit with less *preponderance*," a word presumably borrowed from the French *prépondérance*. It's a deliberate word choice, if a bit unclear in the Dutch, and one that had been translated out of previous editions. My editors, Adam and Ashley Levy, and I discussed it at length. What exactly does she mean here? Is Bea suggesting that she is less important than the other women in Erica's life or is she referring to Erica's level of *absorption* with her? Absorption was, incidentally, the word used in the 1961 translation. Maybe we aren't meant to know. We decided to let the ambiguity speak for itself.

In one of her letters to Manteau, de Jong writes, "The trouble with the translation is that I don't know the Dutch slang anymore. You have to find the equivalents for the American expressions, you can't just translate them literally." She's right, of course, but while working on this book, I found that there were a few cases where a word-for-word translation of a Dutch expression actually presented new lexical possibilities in English. For example, in Chapter 3 when Bea says that Erica was someone who "when she gave you a finger, you wanted a whole hand," she is using a variation of a commonplace Dutch expression, "*als je haar één vinger geeft, neemt zij de hele hand.*" Initially, I tried to translate it with a variation of what de Jong might have considered an English equivalent, for example "when she gave you an inch, you wanted a mile," but it felt off, overly American, and unnecessarily cliché. Or consider the scene in Chapter 5, when Erica describes Judy as "no housecat." Here, the Dutch expression she uses is "*niet voor de poes,*" literally "not for the cat," meaning that she was not to be underestimated, that she could hold her own. I like the way referring to Judy as "no housecat" highlights the contrast between the rule-breaking American divorcée and the two country housewives in the restaurant *and* draws attention to the domestic expectations for women at the time. In both cases, hewing closer to the Dutch yields a more interesting image and better captures the spirit of the original.

It's easy to look at this story through the lens of war or to see it as a lesbian romance that could never be because of the restrictions of the time. But as I got to know Erica and Bea better, I came to see their restlessness, struggles, doubts, and hesitations as reflective of a broader female experience. *The Tree and the Vine* is one of the richest texts I've had the pleasure of translating and one that will stay with me. It is my hope that, with this new translation, the story of Bea and Erica will move readers as it has moved me, that it will push them to think about their own inner worlds and those of the women they love.

DOLA DE JONG (1911–2003) was born Dorothea Rosalie de Jong in Arnhem, The Netherlands. She worked as a dancer and a reporter before she fled the country in 1940. Settling first with her husband in Tangiers, she immigrated to the United States. She was the author of sixteen books for adults and children, including *The Tree and the Vine* and *The Field*, which won the City of Amsterdam Literature Prize in 1947.

KRISTEN GEHRMAN lives in The Hague, The Netherlands. Originally from Charleston, South Carolina, she studied linguistics and literary translation at the University of Lausanne, Switzerland. In addition to her work as a literary translator, she teaches translation, editing, and writing.

Transit Books is a nonprofit publisher of international and American literature, based in Oakland, California. Founded in 2015, Transit Books is committed to the discovery and promotion of enduring works that carry readers across borders and communities. Visit us online to learn more about our forthcoming titles, events, and opportunities to support our mission.

TRANSITBOOKS.ORG